BRINGING ETHAN HOME

Dan Bomkamp

Lovstad Publishing
Poynette, Wisconsin
www.Lovstadpublishing.com

BRINGING ETHAN HOME

ISBN: 0692490353
ISBN-13: 978-0692490358
Previous ISBN: 0692265813

Printed in the United States of America

Cover design by
Lovstad Publishing

DEDICATION

For Dad and Mom.
Together again.

Thanks

I want to thank my publisher and friend Joel Lovstad for the hours he spends on my books and for putting up with me at the many book events we attend together. We make a pretty good team for a couple of old codgers.

BRINGING
ETHAN
HOME

1

Marshall Crawford slipped his sneakers on and called his Boston terrier. "Hey Buzzie, come on let's go buddy!"

The dog came skating around the corner sliding on the wood floor as always on a full run. He jumped up and down and began barking thinking they were going for a run or out to play.

"Sorry Buzz, I gotta go but you can spend the day in the yard. That's better than in the house all day isn't it?"

The dog jumped up and down not knowing what he said but happy to be talked to. Marshall opened the door and let the dog out into the yard adjacent to the patio. The whole area was fenced and the patio was roofed so the dog could play in the grass or on the patio if it got too hot for him. There were padded chairs for him to sleep on and there was a bowl of water for him if he got thirsty.

Marshall picked the little black and white guy up and hugged him. "You be a good boy today and I'll see you when I get back from school."

At the sound of the word school the pup understood what was going to happen. He quit acting like they were going somewhere and settled down. He was used to this and while not happy, he would have a fine day on his own.

"Guard the house," Marshall said as he walked out through the gate toward the neighbor's house.

Marshall's parents, the Crawford's and their neighbors, the

Randall's were not only neighbors but were also best friends and business partners. The dads had been boyhood friends and had gone to college together and ended up back in their hometown buying the local hardware store and going into business together. They'd both met their wives at college and the moms both worked at the family business with their husbands. They'd bought houses side by side in a new subdivision and settled in.

The Randall's son had come first when they had a boy they named Ethan 17 years ago. Then the Crawford's had a son who turned out to be Marshall a little over a year later. The two boys grew up together and although there was a bit over a year difference in age, Ethan had always included Marshall in all of his activities when many older "brothers" would not have much to do with a younger brother.

Marshall crossed the 30 feet to the Randall's house and entered through the back door as he had a thousand times before. Both houses were identical in their size shape and floor plan. They were like many sub-divisions in the country where a builder would start on one end of the block and build a dozen houses in a row, all copies of the first. The only difference was in what kind of siding was on the outside and the color of that siding.

Marshall toed off his sneakers and left them at the door. He walked barefoot across the kitchen and into the recreation room. He grinned as he picked up a ping-pong paddle from the table. He was still grinning as he snuck up the stairs to his best friend's bedroom. He'd gotten up half an hour early so he would have time for his little prank.

When he got to the third step from the top of the stairs, Marshall stepped across it and skipped it. He knew from experience that this step squeaked and he wanted the element of surprise today.

He crossed the hall and opened Ethan's door quietly. A huge smile spread across his face. It was a warm morning and Ethan was stretched out with no blankets covering him. He was lying on his stomach with his arms under his pillows. His feet were hanging over the end of the bed.

Marshall snuck across the room and knelt down by the foot of the bed. He very carefully moved Ethan's feet together taking care not to move either one very much at a time. He didn't want Ethan to wake up. When his feet were right next to each other Marshall reached into his cargo shorts pocket and pulled out an old shoestring. He very carefully looped it around both of Ethan's big toes and then tied a knot in the string.

Ethan didn't move so he tied a second knot just to be sure. Then he quietly moved to the side of the bed away from the side where Ethan was facing and took the ping-pong paddle out of his back pocket. Ethan was wearing red boxers with white polka dots on them. Marshall was nearly laughing out loud when he raised the paddle and smacked it as hard as he could on Ethan's rear-end.

The paddle made a loud crack and Ethan's head snapped up from the pillow. "What the ..."

Marshall ducked down at the foot of the bed.

Ethan reached back and rubbed his rear end.

"What the heck just happened?" he said to himself.

He swiveled his head around and just caught a glimpse of Marshall's head as he ducked below the bed again.

"You little turd! I'm gonna kill you!"

Marshall jumped up screeching with laughter and headed for the door. Ethan swung his feet off the bed to go after him. When he hit the floor he lurched forward because his toes were tied together. His momentum flung him forward and before he had a chance to raise his hands to stop himself, he smashed into the bedroom wall full force with his head. There was a tremendous bang and he slumped to the floor.

Marshall stopped in the hall and listened. He was at the top of the stairs ready to bolt down them. He waited for Ethan to get the string off his toes and come after him. There wasn't a sound in the bedroom.

"He's waiting for me," he thought. "No way I'm going back in there, he'll kill me."

He stood there ready to run for the stairs. No sound came from the bedroom.

Frowning, he listened intently. "He must be having a hard time getting the string off his toes."

He waited for some sound to come from the bedroom but there was nothing but silence.

"He's waiting for me...if I go up there he'll jump me and I'll be toast," he thought.

Several minutes passed. There was no sound from the room. Now he didn't know for sure what to do.

"He didn't get hurt, did he?" he wondered.

Finally he couldn't stand it any longer. He tiptoed back to the door and very slowly opened it. He peeked around the door and got a concerned look on his face. Ethan was lying on the floor out cold. There was a big dent in the drywall in the wall above him where he'd hit his head.

"Oh no," Marshall said. "Oh crap, oh crap."

He hurried across the room and stood there looking down at his friend. He looked like he was sleeping. Marshall checked and could see him breathing so he knew he wasn't dead.

"He must have got knocked out," he said quietly. "I better call 911."

He stood up to get his phone from his pocket and like a striking cobra, Ethan's right hand grabbed Marshall's ankle with a grip like a steel vise.

"Go ahead and call them. Tell them that somebody is about to DIE!"

Marshall began screaming like a ten-year old girl. Not only was Ethan's grip squeezing his ankle to death, he'd nearly peed his pants when he grabbed him.

4

Ethan sat up and began working the shoestring off his toes. In a minute he was free. Marshall had been squirming and pulling trying to get away but Ethan had a grip like an alligator.

"Let me go, it was an accident," he said laughing. "Really I've got to go I'll be late for school."

"Oh you'll be to school on time, maybe a little damp though," Ethan said getting to his feet and picking up Marshall.

"No! Help! Help"

"Yell all you like, there's nobody around little man."

Ethan picked Marshall up like a rag doll and carried him into the bathroom. Marshall grabbed the doorjamb as they went through but couldn't hold on when Ethan pulled.

Ethan turned on the water in the shower and grabbed the top of Marshall's khaki shorts with one hand and his tee shirt with the other and tossed him into the shower. The water was on ice cold. His feet went out from under him and he slid to the shower floor, getting drenched in the ice cold water.

"EEEEeeeeeeeee!" "Help! Help!" Marshall screamed. And then he began to laugh. Ethan joined him laughing and let go of him.

He turned off the water and stood there grinning. "Even?"

Marshall sat there on the floor soaked to the skin and shivering with a grin on his face. He was panting and shaking.

"Yeah, even for now."

2

"Ok, so get out of my shower so I can get ready for school," Ethan said.

Marshall started to step out of the shower but Ethan put a hand on his chest.

"You can't walk through the house dripping wet, take those clothes off."

"What? How am I going to get home?"

"My mom will kill you and me both if you drip water all over the floor. Take your clothes off and leave them in the shower. "I'm not gonna run around the neighborhood naked!"

"Well you should have thought of that before you attacked me. Nobody will see you. You can get your clothes after school. I'll hang them from the shower rod."

"Oh jeez," he said but he did as told. He dropped his shorts and tee shirt and boxers in the bottom of the shower and stepped out. Ethan handed him a towel and he dried off. He turned to lay the towel on the sink and began to laugh. Ethan had dropped his boxers and was bent over adjusting the water temperature in the shower tub. He had a big red spot right in the middle of his butt, just the size and shape of a ping-pong paddle.

"What?" Ethan asked.

"I just noticed your bright red hinder."

Ethan grinned. "Get out of here or there'll be a size 12 footprint on *your* hinder."

Marshall sprinted down the stairs, stopped at the door and picked up his sneakers. He held them in front of his crotch and then ran quickly across the yard to his house. Buzz was happy to see him so soon but he didn't have time to play with the dog. He ran upstairs and put on some dry boxers, some gym shorts and a tee. He said goodbye to Buzz again and ran across the yard to Ethan's pickup, which was in the driveway.

Just as he got there Ethan came out with his book bag. His hair was still wet from the shower.

"I should make you walk," he said getting into the vehicle.

"Oh come on, you got to admit that was a pretty good one," Marshall said grinning.

Ethan had to grin too. "Yeah, but you know, payback is a bitch."

"I'll be on the lookout," Marshall said."

When they got to school they went to their lockers and off to class. Marshall saw Ethan at lunch but he was with a bunch of the baseball team so he didn't go over and sit with them. He knew Ethan would welcome him but he sometimes felt it was better to let him have a little time off with his other friends. They spent most of their time together and he loved every minute of it.

He really couldn't remember when he and Ethan weren't friends. From his first memories as a little kid, Ethan had been a part of everything he'd done. They were in grade school and middle school together even though Ethan was one grade ahead of him. He'd watched his friend grow from a skinny blond kid to a strapping six-foot athlete. Somewhere along the line he'd filled out and turned his skinny frame into a well-muscled body and his shaggy blond hair had begun to curl naturally and framed his handsome face. He let his hair grow to a medium length of blond curls and had the looks that all of the girls took notice of. His green eyes sparkled when he smiled which was often. And even with his good looks, he was modest and friendly with everyone in school. He was easily one of the best athletes in the school but he got along with not only the other athletes but also with the kids who were not considered so cool. He sang in the choir, played trombone in the band and took part in the school plays. If ever there was an all around guy, it was Ethan.

Marshall idolized his friend. They'd been through many adventures and many scrapes. Ethan always looked out for his younger pal and Marshall knew if it came down to it, Ethan would risk his life for him. He knew he surely would do the same.

He was sitting there eating without tasting and thinking about how all the things Ethan and he had been through since they were babies. He'd always been embarrassed to say he loved Ethan but he knew that Ethan knew it, and loved him too. It was like brotherly love only better.

"You coming to practice today?"

Marshall came out of his daydream and looked up to see Ethan smiling at him.

"Did you hear what I just said?" he asked.

"Huh?"

"Where were you?"

Marshall grinned. "I was thinking," he said.

"Are you coming to practice or are you taking the bus home?"

"Oh, I think I'll come to practice, I only have a little homework. I can do it while you play."

"Ok, see you there."

He watched Ethan walk away and grinned. Every girl in the room was watching him with their tongues hanging out. Several of them turned and looked at Marshall with a look like, "You lucky turd!"

After school Marshall packed up his book bag and walked to the baseball field. The team was doing infield practice. Ethan played third base and was clearly one of the best players on the team.

Marshall watched as the coach hit grounders to each position and had them throw to first base. He hit a fiery ground ball to Ethan. Ethan stepped up, caught the ball, took his time, made one long step toward first and fired the ball like it'd come out of a shotgun. The throw was perfect, as his throws always were. That was why they had him on third base. He had an arm like a cannon and very rarely missed getting a runner out.

They practiced and Marshall worked on his geometry homework. A bit later two girls from Ethan's class sat down below him on the bleachers. They were talking and giggling and he heard one of them mention Ethan's name.

He listened as they talked.

"He's so dang good looking," one of them said.

"The best in the whole school," the other said.

"I wonder why he doesn't have a girlfriend?"

"You don't think he does?"

"Have you ever seen him with a girl?"

"Well, no I guess not, but I'm sure he's gone out with girls. I know Cally went to Homecoming with him last year."

"Really? Did she tell you what happened?"

"Not really. She said he was dreamy and a really good dancer and a really good kisser."

"Oh man, I'd like to kiss him."

"I'd like to do more than that."

Marshall giggled when he heard that. The girls turned around.

"Are you listening in on us you little troll?"

Marshall grinned. "My name is Marshall, not troll, and I was sitting here first. If you two ladies want to gossip, do it, but don't expect me to move. And by the way, Ethan is my best friend and I happen to know he likes girls a lot. Just not trampy girls."

"What do you mean trampy girls?"

"Take it for what it's worth. Oh and another thing..." he grinned, "I've seen him in the shower."

The girl's mouths dropped open and he grinned at them.

He got up and walked down the bleachers toward Ethan's pickup. The practice was over and they'd be going home soon.

He turned back and the girls were sitting there staring at him.

Ethan came trotting up and looked at Marshall.

"What's going on?"

"Oh nothing. Those two girls think you're the bomb," he said.

Ethan turned and smiled at the girls. "I don't know them very well," he said.

"Well, they're hot for you."

"Not interested," Ethan said.

"I told them I've seen you naked. I wonder what they'd pay for a picture?"

"You what? Marshall, you little fart...don't even think about it."

3

As they pulled into Ethan's driveway they saw that their parents were home ahead of them. They got out and Marshall started across the lawn to his house.

"Marshall, your parents are here," Ethan's mom said sticking her head out of the front door. "We're cooking out."

"I'll just run home and change," he replied and sprinted across the lawn to his house. He kicked his shoes off and ran upstairs to his room. He put on an old shirt and some older shorts because most cook outs ended in a game basketball. The two boys took on their dads and the game often got a little rough.

Buzz wasn't in the house so he must already be next door, so Marshall ran over and found everyone but Ethan on the patio. A minute later Ethan showed up in some gym shorts and a tank top.

The moms and dads were talking and laughing about something while they cooked and brought food from the kitchen. Buzz was all excited to see his master and ran up to Marshall and jumped up for a scratching of ears.

"Ethan, what happened to your bedroom wall?" his mother asked when she saw him.

"Um, what?"

"The hole in your wall, how did it get there?"

"Well, it's not really a hole, it's more like a little dent," he said.

"It's the size of a soccer ball," his mom said.

"Or someone's head," Marshall said quietly.

"Oh that... I got a cramp when I was getting out of bed and snagged my toe on the sheet and fell over and hit my head on the wall. I didn't think it was so bad. Marshall and I can fix it."

Marshall nodded yes.

"I looked at it and I think it's better to just let it be," his dad said. "By the time we cut the drywall out and patched it we'd probably make it worse."

"Are you sure your head is ok?" his mom asked.

"He's got a real hard head," Marshall said.

Everyone looked at Marshall. Ethan grinned and shook his head.

"Ok, well the burgers are ready."

They all gathered around the table and began to eat. Buzz sat next to Marshall on the bench and enjoyed bites of everything except the coleslaw. He ate most people food but was not a fan of cabbage.

Marshall fed the dog a spoonful of baked beans and he gobbled them down.

"Marshall, don't give Buzz those beans, he farts enough without adding beans to the mix," his dad said.

"But he likes them."

When they were finished they cleaned up the mess and the women went in to wash the dishes.

"So a game of 21?" Ethan's dad asked.

"Old guys against young guys?"

His dad tossed the ball to Ethan. "Take it out, young guy."

The dads were on fire. In no time they were ahead 16 to 10 and it didn't take too long and they won the game. Marshall and Ethan were winded and pretty embarrassed.

"Got time for another?" Marshall's dad asked.

"No, got to study," Ethan said.

"Me too."

The dads retired to the house with a bit of a strut in their steps.

"Jeez, that was pitiful," Ethan said.

"We won't tell anybody. Do you really have to study?"

"Not really but there's a late baseball game I want to watch."

"Ok, well I'll see you in the morning," Marshall said.

"No pranks tomorrow," Ethan warned.

"I promise," Marshall said. He stepped forward and Ethan put his arms around him and they had a good hug.

"See ya," Marshall said and turned and walked home. He always felt good after time spent with the two families and of course Ethan. As much as he loved the guy, he had a prank in mind that would just about make Ethan crazy.

He hurried to his room and was glad to see Ethan's curtains were open. Their rooms were right across the open space of the two houses from each other. They could look out and see each other if they left their curtains open and they did often.

Marshall saw Ethan come into the room with a soda in his hand and sit in his TV chair and prop his bare feet up on a little table. He reached over and picked up his remote and turned on the TV. He searched channels for a bit and found the baseball game that must have been being played on the west coast.

Ethan cracked open his soda and sat back to watch the game. Marshall pulled his curtains almost closed but left a small crack in the middle. Then he went and picked up his own remote. It was the exact make and model of Ethan's. They both had gotten a new TV the previous November when Walmart had their Black Friday Sale. They'd gone and stood in line at midnight to get one of the 40inch wide screen TVs.

Marshall watched and waited. Ethan sipped his soda and burped. Suddenly there was a cheer and a long fly ball was heading for the outfield fence. Ethan sat forward watching the ball as it headed for the outfield wall. Marshall aimed his remote and turned the channel to the Food Network.

"What?? Are you kidding me?" Ethan was rummaging for his remote. He picked it up and switched the channel back to the game. The runner was just crossing home plate.

The announcer came on raving about what a towering hit it had been. "Now let's see that again," he said.

The videotape replay showed the pitcher, the swing and 'Now we'll see how our roast has come out,' Paula Deen was saying as she opened the oven.

"NO!!!" Ethan grabbed his remote and punched it hard changing the channel to again see the runner cross home plate.

"This stupid TV. Damn, I'm taking this thing back... what a piece of junk."

Marshall was laughing so hard he thought he would throw up. He wiped the tears from his eyes and put his remote down. "Enough for one night," he thought to himself.

Just then Buzz curled up by his feet and farted.

"Oh my gosh, Buzzie, you need to go poop."

He rousted the dog and took him out to the yard. Ethan heard him calling the dog and stuck his head out the window.

"Hey Marsh, you ever have trouble with your TV messing up?"

"What do you mean?"

"Mine changes channels on it's own."

"No way. You must have bumped the remote," he replied trying hard to keep a straight face.

"The remote was lying on the table. So yours hasn't ever screwed up?

"Nope."

"Hmm... I think mine is defective."

Marshall shrugged and turned away. He didn't want him to see him laughing like he was.

4

Marshall woke up and sniffed. Buzz was sleeping with him and had farted in his sleep.

"Whew, Buzzie, you stink!" he said to the dog.

Buzz looked up with his flat little face and snorted and he buried his head under the covers and began to snore. Marshall petted the little guy for a while and then got up and hit the shower.

He wiped the mirror off with his towel after he finished and began drying himself off. He looked at his reflection and grinned.

"I'm starting to get a little muscle," he thought to himself. He flexed his biceps a bit and nodded. "Definitely," he said.

He finished drying off and put some deodorant on and then worked his mid-length light brown hair with his fingers giving it a "bed-head" look which was all the rage currently. He'd definitely grown in the past year. He now stood at 5 foot 8 and was up to about 135 pounds. His blue eyes matched his light complexion and his wide white smile. He was glad his mom had insisted on braces when he was younger, looking at his good straight teeth.

"I think in a little while the girls will think I'm cool," he thought. "Of course next to Ethan I'm a troll. But being around him I might get some of his cast-offs." He grinned. "I *am* the king of pranks though," he said out loud.

Ethan had always tried to influence Marshall when it came to school and extracurricular activities. He encouraged him to join the choir and it turned out that he had a very good tenor singing voice. That led Marshall to get involved with the debating team and he'd even been in a couple of the school plays. Ethan always tried to get him to open up and try new things and he was glad he'd listened to him.

Back in his room he pulled on a fresh pair of boxers and some tan cargo shorts and a light blue tee shirt. He looked out the window and saw that Ethan wasn't in bed.

"He must be in the shower," he thought to himself.

An idea he'd had a while back suddenly popped into his head. Did he have time? He decided he did and he sprinted downstairs. Buzz was still under the covers so he left him behind. He hurried into the garage and grabbed the tape dispenser. It was filled with packing tape, the clear, very sticky stuff that was as tough as iron. He went out the garage door and crossed the lawn to Ethan's house and taped the top foot of doorway of the front door with the tape. He stretched it from side to side, strip after strip until he had a foot wide swath of invisible tape across the doorway right from one side doorjamb to the other. The tape was nearly invisible and at about the middle of where Ethan's head would be when he walked out.

Then he ran back home and upstairs to his room. He snuck to the window and looked across. Ethan was in his boxers looking through his dresser for something.

"Hey, how soon are we leaving?" he asked across the gap between the houses.

"Are you ready?"

"I have to take Buzz out and then I will be. I'll meet you in the pickup."

"K."

Marshall woke the little dog up and he lay and yawned and blinked.

"Come on Buzzie, we gotta go," he said trying to hurry the little guy up.

Buzz slowly came to and tried to get back under the covers.

"No, we gotta go buddy, hurry up."

He finally coaxed the dog out of bed and they went downstairs and to the back door where Buzz sprinted off into his enclosure to terrorize some birds that were at the birdfeeder. He opened a jar and got a dog cookie out and gave it to the dog. Then Marshall grabbed his shoes and ran for the pickup barefoot.

"Later Buzzie."

He got to the pickup and got in the passenger side, put on his shoes and waited. He didn't have long to wait. The door opened and Ethan started through the doorway, putting his backpack on as he slammed into the wall of tape.

Ethan's face looked like it had melted as the tape stuck to his nose and mouth and squashed them down. He sprang back from the stretch of the tape and grabbed the barrier with his hands, sticking them too.

"Mhet the pek? Mrshl Mm onna mill yu!"

Tears were running down Marshall's face. He was laughing so hard he thought he'd pee his pants.

Ethan began to try to get loose from the tape and was having a hard time.

"Man't breev! Mrsh. Help!"

Marshall realized both Ethan's mouth and nose were covered with tape. He jumped out of the pickup and ran to the doorway. Ethan was struggling trying to get his hands loose so he could pull the tape off his face. Marshall pulled the tape from the right side of the doorway and began to help him get free. He pulled upward and Ethan yelled as the tape came off his mouth.

"You little shit!"

Now that Ethan could breathe Marshall backed off to a safe distance. Ethan freed his hands and then began to pull the tape off his face.

"Owwwwww!" Ethan screamed as he pulled. He'd freed his nose but now as he pulled the tape off his eyebrows several of the hairs came with it. Then he had his forehead left but a bunch of his hair that was hanging over his brow was now being pulled off with the tape too.

Finally he got it off and looked over at Marshall.

"Are you shitting me? You're going to die Marshall, I'm

going to kill you and put your body in the river and..." He stopped ranting because Marshall was on his back on the driveway laughing so hard he couldn't breathe.

Ethan looked down at the tape.

"Cripes, my eyebrows and hair got pulled out too!"

Marshall laughed all the harder.

Ethan wadded the tape up and threw it at Marshall hitting him in the back of the head.

"Sor....sorry," Marshall gasped. "I didn't think it would pull your hair out. I saw it on TV and it didn't do that."

Ethan stood there shaking his head and then grinned.

"Get in the truck you little dickhead. You better be ready, cause payback is gonna be a bitch!"

Marshall wiped the tears from his face and got in the cab but stayed close to the door. He tried not to smirk but couldn't help it. Ethan backed out of the driveway and they headed down the street to school.

"Are you okay?" Marshall finally asked.

"I'll live..." Ethan said, "but you better prepare."

Marshall grinned and said, "Okay, if you think you can outsmart me, go ahead and try."

He'd soon learn to regret that challenge.

5

Marshall was on guard all the way to school. They'd hardly stopped when he jumped out and sprinted across the parking lot.

"See ya later," he said as he ran.

Ethan just nodded and picked up his backpack out of the bed of the pickup.

"You can bet on it," he said to himself.

The morning passed quickly. Marshall had Phys. Ed. fourth period just before lunch. They went outside and played soccer, which was a sport that he or few of his friends was very good at.

"I don't know how those people in Europe can stand this stupid game," his friend Riley said as he tried to kick the ball and ended up on his back on the ground. Marshall laughed.

"If I had to play this, I'd take up a musical instrument," Riley said as he ran off.

Soon they were told to head to the showers and they all ran into the locker room. Few of them had worked up a sweat so most of them just changed back into their regular clothes. Marshall decided to get a jump on the lunch line and left his gym shorts and gym shirt on. He did the same thing most days and it worked so he got to the front of the line most of the time. He figured to eat first and then run back and change before his next class. As soon as the bell rang he sprinted down the hall and got into line.

"What's on the menu today?" he asked the kid ahead of him.

"Dunno, I think some soup and sandwich thing."

The line was moving slowly forward and Marshall saw Ethan walking down the hallway with a couple of his friends. Ethan turned and said something to his buddies and they grinned as they walked past.

"Hey Turd, how's it going?" Ethan said.

"Okay, how's your face feel? They say that exfoliation thing is good for your complexion."

Ethan grinned. "I'll live I think."

"Good, sorry I didn't think it'd pull your eyebrows out you know."

"Don't worry, I still have most of them."

Ethan proceeded down the hallway and got into line with his friends. Soon Marshall turned the corner and made it into the lunchroom. It was a big open room with lines of tables along both sides and a wide aisle down the center. There were kids sitting at the tables in little groups. Lunch groups consisted of kids from the same grade, or from certain clicks, like the band kids, the jocks and the burnouts. Marshall saw some of his buddies at the other end of the room.

He went through the line and it was indeed soup and sandwich day. He chose a turkey sandwich and beef vegetable soup. He proceeded down the line and got a bowl of pudding and a carton of chocolate milk.

He was concentrating pretty hard on not spilling his soup as he walked down the middle aisle towards his buddies. They were talking animatedly about something and he was looking forward to getting into the conversation. Suddenly he saw one of his buddies look up and get a concerned look on his face. The kid nudged the guy on his left and he too looked up and got a surprised look on his face.

Marshall wondered what they were looking at behind him when he felt hands on the sides of his gym shorts. He didn't have time to set his tray down or try to run as his shorts were jerked down to his ankles instantly. He looked down and to his horror he saw his boxers were lying on the floor with the shorts. He waddled as fast as he could to the nearest table so he could set his tray down. Then he bent over to pull his pants up.

Just as he grabbed his boxers and shorts, he felt something cold and wet in his butt crack. He turned to see Ethan running in the other direction holding a mustard squeeze bottle.

He felt his backside and it was full of mustard. He pulled his shorts up in front and ran across the cafeteria while the whole place laughed and yelled at him.

Marshall headed for the locker room and just as he was nearly there the gym coach came out the door.

"Marshall did you forget something?"

Marshall was holding his shorts up over his front but his whole rear end was sticking out and his crack was full of mustard.

"Nothing coach, I just decided I need a shower." And he sprinted past the surprised teacher.

Thankfully the locker room was empty. Marshall took off his shoes and socks and then his shorts and boxers. Then he took off his shirt and ran to the shower. He turned on the water and backed under it letting the hot water run down his back. He looked at the floor and the water was bright yellow. He had a grin on his face as he scrubbed himself clean.

"That was a good one," he thought to himself. "This is war now... Ethan will pay!"

By the time he got dried off and dressed his soup was cold. When he came walking into the cafeteria everyone clapped and cheered. He looked over and saw Ethan at a table with his pals. Ethan saluted him.

Marshall just nodded. He mouthed the words, "Good one."

Ethan bowed.

6

There was a baseball game after school so Marshall went to the field and climbed up on the bleachers to watch it. The teams were both already on the field and Ethan's team was taking batting practice. He watched as Ethan smacked three pitches in a row deep into center field. Dang he was a good hitter.

Soon one of his buddies climbed up next to him and sat down.

"Nice show today," he said grinning.

"Jeez, do you think anybody saw my wiener?" Marshall asked.

"Only the whole school," the kid answered.

"Oh man."

The kid laughed. "Some of the girls were pretty impressed," he said.

"Really? They said that?" Marshall asked.

"One person asked me if I had your phone number," the kid said.

"Which one?"

"Don't know the name. That guy in the freshman class with the ponytail... you know the one who plays flute? He asked me where you lived."

"What?"

The kid began to laugh. "Just kidding."

Just then Marshall's phone played "On Wisconsin". He answered it.

"Marshall, it's Mom, we're going out for pizza with the Randall's after work, so why don't you and Ethan meet us at the Dug Out?"

"Ethan's playing a game you know."

"Yes we know. That's why we decided on doing this. If the game runs long we old folks will just have another pitcher of beer while we wait."

Marshall grinned. His parents didn't drink much but once in a while they had a few beers and occasionally his mom and Ethan's mom got a little silly.

"Okay, make sure to get one pepperoni at least," he said.

"Okay honey, see you then."

The game started and a little over an hour later the last out was made. Ethan, as usual, played like a professional. His fielding was perfect and he hit two singles and one fly ball.

Marshall waited at the pickup for his friend and soon Ethan came out of the locker room in his school clothes and joined him.

"Our parents are at the Dug Out and we're having pizza for dinner," Marshall said.

"Cool, I'm starved."

They drove across town to the pizza joint and found their parents sitting at a large table with room for two more. After talking about the game and other things for a while Marshall's dad asked the boys if they had plans for the upcoming Saturday.

They both shook their heads no.

"Why?" Marshall asked.

"We thought the four of us could go fishing," Ethan's dad said.

"Don't you have to work?" Ethan asked.

"We can't work all the time. We haven't been fishing for a long time. I got a hot tip that the walleyes are biting up at the dam and I thought it'd be fun for us to spend a day together. After all next week we're heading to Canada on our annual trip, so we wanted to spend some time with you and Marshall before we go."

The two dads had been boyhood friends like Ethan and Marshall were now. When they graduated from high school they both went to the same college and shared a house with two guys from Iowa. The four of them became great pals. When they graduated, Ethan and Marshall's dads both became Marines. Military service was kind of a tradition in both families so they did their duty and spent 4 years in the service of their country. After their service the two friends re-connected with their friends from college and took their first fishing vacation to Canada. They'd gotten together every spring from then on and taken a fishing trip together..

"This is our 20th year of our annual trek and we're going all out," Ethan's dad explained.

"Yeah, we're going to fly in to a remote lake and have it all to ourselves. There's only one cabin on the lake so just a few fishermen use it each year. The brochure shows strings of huge walleyes, northern and small mouth bass." He passed a fold out brochure and the boys looked at the pictures.

"Wow, that looks great," Marshall said.

"And here's the best part. If it turns out to be as good as they say, we're going to book a second trip in June for the four of us."

"You mean Ethan and me?" Marshall said excitedly.

"That's exactly what I mean."

The boys were very excited. "I've never flown in a plane before," Marshall said.

"Holy cow that sounds great Dad," Ethan said.

"But can you be away from the store for so much time?"

"Ethan, the store is doing very well. Financially we're in very good shape. We have great employees and your moms will still be there running things. You know, you and Marshall are getting to the age where soon you'll be off to college or a job someplace and we think it's time to spend as much time with you as we can."

"Time goes by quickly," Marshall's dad said, "it seems like the two of us were just kids like you a short time ago and here we are middle aged with almost adult kids of our own."

The boys were very excited about the prospect of a trip to Canada and a week of fishing with their fathers.

The pizzas came and they all dove in. Ethan and Marshall both had huge grins on their faces as they ate.

When they were all done, Marshall and Ethan left in Ethan's pickup and the parents drove home together.

"That's about the coolest thing I've heard in a while," Ethan said. "The way the fishing is in Canada, even a rookie like you might catch a fish."

Marshall nodded. "Go ahead," he said, "you'll eat your words Saturday."

Ethan looked over and grinned.

7

Friday after school the boys loaded the boat with all the fishing gear. Ethan's dad, Brian actually owned the boat and they kept it in his garage but Marshall's dad, Tim had bought most of the extra gear like a fish finder and trolling motor so they both owned it. They'd hardly ever gone fishing without each other so there was not much need for each of them to own a boat. It was a large extra wide 16-foot flat-bottom with a 50 HP motor on it, so there was plenty of room for the four of them.

That evening they made sandwiches and got everything ready and set their alarms for 6 am. The boys were much more energized when they woke than on a day they went to school and it didn't take long for everyone to arrive at the garage. They loaded the lunch into the boat, hooked it to the trailer hitch and all piled into Brian's Pathfinder.

"Dad is it okay if Buzz comes along?" Marshall asked.

"Will he sit still?"

"He'll be good. He might be a little excited at first but he'll calm down."

"Okay, bring him along."

Marshall ran home and got the dog, who was jumping up and down like crazy and very happy to go for a ride in the car.

"Are we going up to the dam?" Ethan asked as they headed out of town to the north.

"Yeah, the walleyes are running and the word is they're getting some nice ones," his dad answered.

They stopped in the next town for bait at a little shop and then walked across the street to a restaurant and had a huge breakfast. Marshall wrapped up a few pieces of bacon in a napkin for Buzz. Then they drove the rest of the way to the boat landing.

At the landing they all got out and Tim checked the boat to be sure the plug was in and then climbed up into it. The boys took the straps off and Tim tipped up the motor. Brian backed down to the landing and backed in until the boat was just ready to float off the trailer. Tim lowered the motor and started it and then Brian backed the rest of the way and the boat floated free. Brian parked the vehicle and met the boys on a little dock that stuck out into the river. They waited for Tim to pull up in the boat and all stepped aboard.

Buzz was sniffing around on the shore and Marshall called him. The little dog came on a dead run and jumped into the boat with great enthusiasm.

"Does he know enough to stay in the boat?" Tim asked.

"We'll see," Marshall said.

"You might as well drive as long as you're back there," Brian said.

"You just want to get a minnow on your jig on the way up to the dam so you have an advantage over me," Tim said grinning.

Brian laughed. "You know me pretty well."

"I should, we've been doing this since we were the same age as these boys."

Ethan smiled at Marshall. It was nice to see how well their dads got along after being friends for so long. He hoped he and Marshall would be such good friends twenty years from now too.

They arrived at the dam and slowed down. Brian pointed to an area that was less congested. "Let's start there," he said.

There were about 40 other boats at the dam but it was a large area and everyone kept alert so they didn't get too close to other fishermen.

"Obviously your hot tip on the fishing wasn't a secret," Ethan said to his dad.

"Obviously, but I'm sure there are enough fish for all of us."

"Okay, you guys know the rules," Tim said, "last one to catch his first fish buys the beer."

"Huh?" Marshall said.

"Soda for you guys, beer for the old guys," Tim said.

"You're on," both the boys said in unison.

The fishing was pretty intense from then on. They each baited up a lead head jig and dropped it over the side to the bottom. Then they reeled up so the jig was just inches above the bottom and twitched it trying to entice a walleye to bite it. There was no talking or joking... it was serious business.

Tim got the first bite. He let out a whoop and set the hook and fought a medium size walleye to the boat. He had a big grin on his face as he took it off the hook and put it in the live well.

"I'm not buying," he said.

Just then Marshall felt a tic on his line and set the hook. He felt the fish on the line fighting but just as quickly as it was on, it came off again.

"Dang, slipped off," he said reeling up to re-bait.

Brian set his hook and turned and grinned at the boys as he reeled up a small walleye.

"You're not going to count that little thing are you?" Ethan asked.

"There is no size requirement," his dad said. "I am going to release it though."

He tossed the fish over the side and smirked.

"Looks like the younger generation is buying."

Ethan and Marshall were both concentrating hard when Marshall's line suddenly started peeling off the reel. He reared back and set the hook and his drag began to scream as line was pulled into the water.

"Holy smokes I've got a whale!" he yelled.

Ethan set his hook and fought a walleye to the top and turned to Marshall, "You buy little man."

"Not fair, I hooked this fish before you did, I just don't have it up yet."

"Tough luck pal," Ethan said laughing.

"Marshall, what have you got hold of there?" his dad asked.

"I don't know Dad but you better start the motor and follow it, my reel is almost empty of line."

Marshall's line trailed off into the water straight toward the dam. It was being pulled off the reel steadily and there wasn't much left.

"Hurry up or I'm gonna lose all my line," he said excitedly.

Tim started the motor and began to follow the line. Marshall moved to the front of the boat and reeled as he gained on the fish.

"I think it's getting tired," he said.

Brian looked back at Tim. "I don't think you're even close to landing it Marshall... not even close."

Suddenly the fish turned from the dam and started across the front of it toward the shore. Tim turned and followed.

"It's gotta be a world record walleye," Marshall said.

The dads laughed.

8

They followed the fish from one side of the river to the other. Then they went downstream for half a mile and then back up toward the dam. Other fishermen in other boats got out of the way as they approached knowing what Marshall was fighting.

"This can't be a walleye," Marshall finally said after nearly half an hour.

"You're right about that," Brian said.

"What is it?"

"I think it's probably a paddlefish," his dad said.

"A what?"

"It's a paddlefish Marshall, they call them spoonbills too. They congregate here in the spring to spawn. They're a very old fish that's been around for millions of years. They get pretty big and I think you have one of those big ones. Just take your time. It'd be fun to see it at least."

"Can we keep it if I catch it?"

"No son, they don't have an open season. We'll have to put it back if you catch it."

Ethan was watching the water and suddenly he shouted, "I saw it, oh my gosh, it's huge, it looks like a shark!"

Marshall reeled down to the water and raised up his rod and suddenly the water swirled and there was the biggest fish he'd ever seen other than in a TV show. It was six feet long and heavy bodied with a long snout that stuck out from a huge mouth.

"Holy Moley! What the heck?"

The fish dove again and peeled off a lot of Marshall's line. He worked and worked and soon it was at the surface again.

"It's tired out," his dad said.

Just then there was a blur of black and white and Buzz jumped over the side of the boat onto the back of the huge fish. It dove again and Buzz was left dogpaddling in the water.

"Buzzie! What the heck are you doing?"

Ethan began to coax the little dog back toward the boat and he grabbed him and pulled him aboard.

"You're pretty brave little man, that fish weighs ten times as much as you do."

The dog shook off and peered over the side into the water.

"Ethan get in the bow and see if you can grab its snout, I'll grab the tail," Brian said.

Ethan looked at his dad, "Grab the snout? Are you sure?"

"It's perfectly safe, these things are plankton eaters… they don't have any teeth."

Ethan didn't look too sure but did as he was told. Marshall raised the fish again. He reached over the side and took hold of the long snout. It was kind of shaped like a skateboard but not as wide. His dad grabbed the tail.

"Ok, one, two, three, lift!"

The two of them hoisted the fish from the water and laid it in the bottom of the boat.

"Oh my gosh, it IS a shark!" Marshall said.

The two dads laughed.

"No it's as old as the sharks but this guy wouldn't hurt you a bit. Brian opened the mouth and it was huge.

"See they swim through the water with this big mouth open and filter out plankton and other little critters from the water. That's all they eat, plankton and microscopic organisms."

"What's the big snout for?" Ethan said examining the big flat appendage.

"It has sensors on it to locate food I guess," his dad said.

"Look at all the jigs hooked into it," Marshall said.

The fish had at least a dozen other jigs besides Marshall's embedded in its sides and tail.

"Take a pliers and pull them out carefully. Then we'll get a picture and put this old guy back into the river," Tim said.

The boys cleaned up the fish and Tim asked a boat close by

to take a picture for him. They moved close and he handed his camera across and then the boys got in the middle and held the body of the fish up while the dads got on each end and held the tail and snout. They all said "cheese" and the other fisherman snapped a picture.

"Okay, let's put the guy back and let him go in peace."

They carefully lowered the fish into the water. Brian held onto his snout and moved him back and forth through the water, reviving him. When he began to move his fins and tail, Brian let go and the fish swam off out of sight.

"Holy smokes, that was something," Marshall said.

"You did a good job of playing him," his dad said.

"A lot of people pulled too hard and were too impatient and that's where all those other jigs came from."

Marshall had a big grin on his face.

"Well, guess I have to buy the beer," he said, "but it's worth it to catch a fish like that. Plus I got a dozen new jigs for free."

They went back to fishing and spent a memorable day on the water. The fish bit, the lunch was tasty and all in all it was a day they'd all remember for a long time. Buzzie was fascinated with the fish in the live well and stood with his head looking over the edge and grabbed at one now and then trying to catch it. When they loaded up at the end of the day they had a dozen nice walleyes that would make a great fish fry when they got home.

They stopped at a small grocery to get some beer for the fish fry. Marshall got his wallet out but his dad stopped him.

"I'll get it. You caught the fish of the day, it wouldn't be fair to make you buy.'

Marshall winked. "Thanks Dad," he said.

Dang, how lucky he was to have such a great dad and great friends. Life was good.

Buzz slept all the way home. He was used to napping all day and his big adventure on the water tired the little guy out completely.

9

Monday morning Marshall had a hard time getting out of bed. Buzz was snoring under the covers and he felt like ignoring his alarm clock. Finally he decided he had to move, so he reached over and shut the alarm off. He sat on the edge of the bed and yawned and stretched. Under the covers Buzz snorted and then began snoring again. He looked down at the lump in the blankets.

"You're not a morning person are you Buzzie?" He smiled and patted the lump. The dog ignored him. "If we wanted to take you squirrel hunting we'd have to put you in a backpack and carry you to the woods, you lazy boy." The dog kept snoring.

Marshall stood up and looked out the window. Ethan's window was open and his bed was empty.

"He must be showering or downstairs already," he thought to himself as he padded to the bathroom. He stepped inside and shut the door. He yawned as he peed, then flushed and dropped his boxers to the floor. He turned to the shower and pulled open the curtain.

Suddenly a blast of ice-cold water hit him in the face and body.

"Whaaaa?" he yelled.

Then a cloud of white powder hit him. Being wet, the powder stuck to him making him look like the Pillsbury Doughboy. The white powder smelled and tasted like flour.

His eyes were clamped shut but he heard laughter and opened them blinking the flour away. Ethan was standing barefoot and shirtless, in his shower wearing his swimsuit holding an empty ice cream pail and an empty plastic glass.

"You, you, what the heck?" Marshall gasped.

Ethan stepped up to Marshall and put the ice cream pail over his head and walked from the room.

"Remember this the next time you consider pulling a prank on me," he said with a laugh.

Marshall stood there covered in wet flour. He took the bucket off his head. At first he was really pissed but then he turned and saw himself in the mirror. He grinned and his teeth showed through the flour mask.

"That was a pretty good one," he said. Then he looked down at the mess on the floor. "Oh man, I gotta get this showered off me and clean up the floor or mom will kill me."

He stepped into the shower and closed the curtain and cleaned himself off. The flour made a paste and it took a lot of scrubbing to get it all off. He got out and stepped carefully across the mess on the floor and took his towel out into the bedroom and dried off. He put on his boxers and went to the kitchen to get a mop and pail. It took a while to clean up all the mess but he finished, dressed and ran downstairs, let Buzz out and ran across the yard to where Ethan was waiting in his pickup.

He jumped in the passenger seat.

"Good one," he said.

Ethan nodded. "I saw that on MTV."

"I'm going to have to start watching that I guess."

Ethan grinned and backed them out of the driveway.

"We've got a game tonight, are you coming to watch?" he asked.

"Yeah, I'm planning on it," Marshall said.

They pulled up to the school and Marshall noticed Ethan tossed his athletic bag into the front seat from the back of the pickup.

"This thing takes up my whole locker," he said. "I'm gonna leave it here, and get it after school."

"Good idea," Marshall said. The wheels were turning in his head. An idea was forming.

When he got to this locker, Marshall got his notebook and closed the locker. His pal Randy was just walking up.

"Going to English?" Randy asked.

"Yup, let's go."

They walked toward the classroom. Randy looked at Marshall and then looked again.

"What ya lookin at?" Marshall asked.

"What's that in your ear?"

Marshall dug into his ear with his pinkie finger and came out with a big gob of flour paste.

"It's flour," he said.

"Why do you have flour in your ear?"

"I put it on my face before I shower, it makes my skin soft."

Randy looked at him not knowing if he was pulling his leg or not.

"Serious?"

Marshall grinned. "No Ethan pranked me this morning but I'm working on a plan to get him back at the baseball game today."

Randy grinned. "Ethan? Won't he be mad?"

"I hope so," Marshall said.

10

Marshall's next class was chemistry and he made his way to the classroom as quickly as he could. He needed a nerd.

He walked into the room and checked the back corner and was glad to see three of the smart kids who were a bit "odd" standing in a tight circle talking. Marshall walked up and one of the kids looked up at him.

"Hey Marshall, what's up?"

"I need you guys to help me with a prank," he said.

They all turned with expectant grins on their faces.

"Like what kind of prank?"

The kid wore glasses and had braces and shoulder length hair.

"I want to put a package of something that looks like poop in the back of one of the baseball players white uniform pants so it breaks open during the game and it looks like he crapped his pants."

They all looked surprised.

"Wow, when is this going to happen?"

This was a short kid with red hair that looked like it had never been combed.

"After school today."

The three kids looked at each other.

The third kid, a heavy-set kid with curly brown hair looked at the first two.

"We could use a glassine envelope and perforate the top so when pressure was put on it the fake poop would ooze out."

"Yeah or maybe a straw, but that would probably break too soon.'

"Anyone got a pudding cup?"

"Yeah, but its butterscotch."

"That'd do but I'm sure we can find a chocolate someplace."

Marshall stood there listening and liking what he was hearing.

"So you think you can work it out?" he asked.

"No problem. Who are you pranking?"

"Ethan."

They all looked alarmed. "Ethan Randall? Jeez he's like a god, are you sure he won't take us all out and kill us?"

Marshall laughed. "Ethan and I are best friends. We prank each other all the time. He's not a typical jock that is good looking. He's really a good guy. Oh, he'll be pissed for a bit but he'll think it's funny too."

"You're sure? I'd hate to spend the rest of the year with Ethan pounding me on the head every day," the little redhead said.

"Don't worry. It'll be cool."

"Ok, so where are these pants?" the longhaired kid asked.

"They're in Ethan's pickup. I'll run and get them at lunch. Can you have this ready by then?"

The three boys nodded. "We'll meet you in the locker room at noon."

They all bumped fists and went to their seats as the bell rang.

Marshall couldn't help but grin as he thought about this amazing prank.

At noon he sprinted out to the parking lot and dug Ethan's white baseball uniform pants out of his bag. He wadded them up and hid them in his backpack and ran to the locker room.

He burst in the door and the three boys almost had a heart attack.

"Jeez, you scared us to death," the redhead said.

"I've got the pants."

The boys took the pants and turned them inside out. They grinned as they looked at the back seam.

"Good this is going to work perfect."

There was extra material on each side of the seam left over when the seam was sewed. The tall kid carefully took a long clear tube from his backpack. It was filled with brown liquid.

"This is a glassine tube. It's kind of a plastic that is used for storing liquids. We made this one long and thin and left the top three inches empty. At the very top the seam it's paper-thin but it's sealed."

Marshall nodded that he understood.

"This is a squib. It's a little charge that they use when they make a movie or a play that can be set off remotely when a gun shoots to simulate blood. We'll attach it to the glassine envelope and when we set it off it will break the seal and the pudding will run out. We'll stitch it into the left over material in the crotch at the back of the pants."

"Where did you get that squib thing?"

"We all are stage hands for the school plays. None of us is cool enough to be in the play but we have access to all kinds of cool stuff."

"So then whenever we want, we can set it off?"

The three nodded.

Marshall was grinning from ear to ear.

"And it'll look like he crapped his pants," he said smiling widely.

The three boys nodded. "Exactly," one of them said.

"I like it... I like it a lot."

The three worked the pudding straw into the seam and one came out with a little sewing kit and carefully stitched the thing under the extra material. When they were done you couldn't tell anything was there. They turned the pants back outside out and carefully folded them up.

"Okay, put them back. There's a chance he might break it when he puts them on but these tubes are pretty tough."

"So do you think it will work?" Marshall asked.

"I guarantee it," the tall longhaired kid said.

The three of them stood there grinning.

"You guys rock," Marshall said.

"Nerds rule," the tall kid replied.

"See you at the game?" Marshall asked.

"Wouldn't miss it," he replied. "Well bring the activator for the squib with us."

Marshall sprinted out to the parking lot and carefully put the pants back into the gym bag. His stomach was grumbling because he missed lunch but he was really looking forward to the game today.

11

The final bell rang and Marshall ran to his locker to gather up his books and backpack. He walked to the baseball field and the team was already out running drills. Ethan was on third base fielding grounders and throwing to first. He waved at Marshall when he saw him. Marshall waved back.

Two girls sitting on the bleachers saw him wave and looked at Marshall.

"You know Ethan?" one asked.

"Yup," Marshall replied.

"He's so hot," the other one said.

Marshall grinned. "You think he's good looking?"

"Oh yeah, he's the most beautiful boy in the school."

"I guess he's okay," Marshall said.

"How come he knows you?" the first girl asked. She looked at him like he was a dead squirrel on the road.

"We're best friends. He lives next door and we do all kinds of stuff together."

"You two are best friends?"

"Yup."

"You're the luckiest little troll in the school," the girl said.

"Troll! That's not nice. I was going to tell you about Ethan getting into the shower but now I'm hurt." Marshall began walking off.

"Wait, wait, don't go we were kidding."

Marshall just grinned and kept walking. He climbed up to the top seats of the bleachers where the three guys who'd helped him were sitting. One had a pair of binoculars and the other was doing something on a cell phone. They slid over so Marshall could sit with them.

"You know those girls?" one asked.

"Nope. They saw Ethan wave to me and were pumping me

for information about the most beautiful boy in the school."

They all laughed. The kid with the binoculars said, "He is pretty good looking."

They all looked at him.

"What? I was just stating the obvious."

Soon both teams were in their dugouts and the game started. The visiting team was up to bat first. Their first hitter struck out. The second hitter hit a hard grounder between third and shortstop and Ethan made a fantastic catch and threw the guy out.

The kid with the binoculars checked out Ethan's pants. He looked up.

"Nope."

The next hitter smacked a long ball into deep center field. He rounded second base and headed for third as the throw came in from the outfield. Ethan guarded the base, took the throw and the hitter slid into the base. There was a cloud of dust but when it had cleared the runner was out and Ethan was dusting off his uniform.

The kid with the binoculars checked his butt. "Nope."

"It's holding up okay but we better not push our luck," one kid suggested.

"You don't suppose he found it," the redhead said.

"He would have said something to me," Marshall replied.

"Give it time," the longhaired kid said. "I guarantee my work."

Ethan's team was up to bat. The first batter grounded out and the second struck out.

"Our hitting is a bit lacking," the longhaired kid said.

The next batter got up and hit a nice single to left field. Then it was Ethan's turn to bat.

He strode up to the plate and took a couple of practice swings. The kid with the binoculars looked at his butt.

"I can see the outline of the straw, it's still there."

Ethan swung on the first pitch and hit a long fly ball to deep right/center field. He took off running to first and rounded the bag and set out for second. The throw was on the way so Ethan slid and when the dust cleared he was called safe.

"Do it now," Marshall said.

The heavy kid took a little box from his pocket. He grinned and pushed a button on it.

"Done," he said.

Ethan got up from the infield and brushed off the front of this pants and uniform shirt. Then he bent over to tie his shoe.

"Oh My God!" the kid with the binoculars said.

They didn't need binoculars to see the brown streak down the back of Ethan's white pants. It looked like he'd pooped his pants when he slid. The whole bleachers began to hum with people pointing and laughing.

Ethan looked up and got a frown on his face. He put his hand behind him and felt the back of his pants. His eyes got huge as he felt the wetness.

"Time!" he yelled to the umpire.

The ump called time and Ethan ran to the dugout. You could hear the laughter coming from his teammates and the crowd. Suddenly his face appeared at the doorway to the dugout and he looked right at Marshall.

"Uh oh," Marshall said.

Ethan came out of the dugout on a run, headed right for the bleachers. Marshall went over the back of them and took off running for the street. Ethan followed him for a block and then gave up and walked back to the game. He was greeted by a lot of laughter and cheers.

"It's pudding," he said loudly.

That only made things worse.

He stood there with a half grin on his face. "That little fart," he thought, "that was a good one but now I've got to come up with the prank of the year."

Marshall walked all the way home and then stood guard watching for Ethan to get home. He wanted to be sure to know where Ethan was at all times for the next few days. He knew there'd be retaliation but that was part of the fun.

About an hour later Ethan pulled into the driveway. Marshall looked out the window as Ethan came into his room. He looked across at Marshall and grinned.

"Good one," he said.

"Thank you."

"You know you must die now."

"I expected as much."

12

Friday came and the two families went out to their favorite bar for the Friday Night Fish Fry. The place was packed as it usually was because they had the best fish in town. They got drinks, beers for the grownups and Cokes for Ethan and Marshall and stood talking while they waited for a table.

When they were seated they talked about the two dads having to rise early the next morning for their annual trip to Canada.

"We're picking up the other guys on the way," Marshall's dad said. "All we have to take is our fishing gear and food and drinks. Everything else is provided. Then we load up and the pilot flies us into the lake."

"How many others will be there?" Ethan asked.

"Just the four of us," his dad said. "There is only one cabin on the lake. We'll have it all to ourselves."

"Well, don't catch all the fish," Marshall said, "Leave a few for June when we get there."

"I'm sure there'll be plenty left for you guys. If it doesn't pan out to be good fishing we'll shop around and find another lake for us to try in June. Either way the four of us will spend a week together in Canada this year."

"Maybe it can be the first of a yearly vacation," Ethan's dad added.

"That'd be good," Marshall said nodding his head.

The next morning the whole family was up early in both houses to see the dad's off on their trip. Ethan hugged his dad and Marshall did the same and then they traded dads and hugged again.

"See you in a week," they said as they drove off.

"Well, now we're up, what is there to do?" Ethan asked.

"Go back to bed," Marshall said.

"Oh come on, let's do something."

"Like what?"

"Let's take a bike ride."

"To where?" Marshall asked.

"I don't know we'll just start riding and see where we get to."

Marshall shook his head.

"Did you get a baseball to the head yesterday after I left?"

Ethan laughed. "Get your bike."

They started out riding toward the edge of town and then went down the highway toward the next town.

"How far are we going?"

"Remember that little diner about half way down this road?" Ethan asked.

"Yeah, you want to go that far?"

"Oh don't be so lazy, that's only 8 or 9 miles. They say that diner makes the best breakfast in the area, let's go and have breakfast there."

"You got money?"

"Of course."

"You buying?"

Ethan grinned. "If you beat me there, I'll buy."

Marshall stood up and began pedaling like mad. They were going as fast as they could as they went around curves and up and down hills. It didn't take many minutes and the diner was in sight. Ethan really began working hard and pulled up along side Marshall.

"No way!" Marshall rode like he'd never ridden before. They were less than a block away when he pulled out in front. He came to a dust raising halt as he put his brakes on in the gravel parking lot with Ethan right behind him.

Ethan fanned the dust away. "You win little man." He had a huge grin on his face.

"Did you let me win?" Marshall asked breathing heavily.

"Nope."

Ethan was barely breathing hard. He put his arm around his younger buddy.

"Come on little man, let's get some vittles."

The two friends went into the diner and had a huge breakfast of pancakes, eggs, bacon and hash browns.

"You're going to have to strap me to your bike and take me back," Marshall said patting his belly.

"We'll go slow," Ethan said smiling.

"Okay, I guess that'll work."

Ethan walked up to pay for the food and Marshall watched him. "Dang, what would I do without him for a friend?" he thought to himself.

13

The week passed quickly. Ethan had a baseball game after school on Thursday and Marshall was there in the bleachers watching with his "geek" friends.

"So was Ethan really mad about the pudding?" the little redheaded kid asked.

Marshall laughed. "He acted like he was mad but he finally admitted it was a very well done prank," he said. "The problem is that I know he's cooking up something to get me back."

The boys all laughed and began speculating about the retaliation.

"You should strike again right away," the tall skinny kid suggested. "He won't expect another prank so soon."

Marshall grinned. "I think I better lay off for a while. But if you guys come up with something good, let me know."

The moms were going to a musical that night so Marshall and Ethan had to fend for themselves. When they got home they changed into shorts and tees and fired up the grill to cook some burgers. Buzzie was at his glory having both his master and his second master with him. Ethan loved the little dog nearly as much as Marshall did.

After they'd eaten and cleaned up the grill they settled down and watched a movie on TV. They were watching a movie about aliens invading Los Angeles and a bunch of Marines defending it.

"Jeez those guys have no fear," Marshall said after an exciting scene.

"I think it's a lot like that for real too," Ethan said. "Dad always talks about their days in the service and how they're like a brotherhood. It's a pretty tight bunch of guys."

"What are you going to do next year?" Marshall asked.

"I'm not sure," Ethan replied. "I'd like to start college but I also think I want to go into the Marine Crops."

"Really? You're going into the military?"

"I'm not sure Marsh, I don't know for sure what I want to do with my life. If I spend a few years in the Marines, I'll have time to find out what I want to do afterward."

Marshall nodded. "That makes sense, but aren't you afraid?"

"What of getting killed?"

"Yeah, that or getting hurt? Doesn't that scare you a little?"

"I'd be lying if I said it didn't bother me, but I guess I'm willing to take the chance."

They sat quietly for a long time. Ethan looked over at his younger buddy and he could see Marshall was on the verge of crying. He slid over and put his arm around Marshall's shoulder and pulled him to his side.

"Hey don't worry little man, I'll be careful."

Marshall's eyes filled with tears. "Yeah, I know, but I'm sure gonna miss you when you leave," he said.

"I'll miss you too, but we'll always be friends, whether I'm next door or a long way away. I expect we'll be old middle aged guys like our dads are now, and going fishing together in the future."

Marshall smiled at that. "You promise?"

"I promise Marshall," he said.

14

Late Saturday evening the dads pulled into the driveway at Ethan's house. The boys and moms had been waiting for them and everyone hurried out to the driveway to hear about the fishing trip.

The two dads were dead tired from the long drive home but filled with exciting stories about the fish they'd caught, the plane ride into and back from the lake, and the animals they'd seen in the outpost cabin.

"The place is like going back in time," Ethan's dad said. "The cabin is a box made of plywood with a corrugated tin roof. The refrigerator and stove run on gas and the heater is a 55 gallon oil drum that's been converted into a wood burning stove."

"How was the fishing?" Marshall asked excitedly.

"Fantastic!" his dad replied. "We caught so many walleyes and northern that we almost got tired of fishing... almost."

They talked late into the evening and the dads told the boys that they'd booked the same cabin for a week in exactly one month. The boys were excited and both could hardly get to sleep that night.

Sunday morning the two families went to church together and when they got home Ethan suggested that they go fishing. The dads had a lot of catch-up work to do so they declined but Ethan and Marshall decided to go on their own. All the talk of fishing had them excited and a day on the water would help with that.

They decided to take the little flat bottom boat they used for fishing the small ponds in the river bottoms. They loaded the boat in the back of Ethan's pickup and each grabbed a fishing rod and reel and their tackle boxes. They decided to take Buzzie along since he behaved pretty well the last time in the boat.

After a short drive through the dirt roads of the bottoms,

they stopped at a slough that had always been one of their favorites. Ethan backed up to the edge of the high-bank and they slid the boat out of the pickup and down over the bank to the slough.

Ethan moved the pickup away from the "landing" and Marshall carried their tackle down and put it into the boat. They were both wearing shorts and tee shirts and they took off their shoes and left them on the shore. Marshall got into the front of the boat, called Buzz and he jumped in and sat beside him. Ethan pushed off and jumped in once they were away from the bank. They took paddles and began paddling the boat toward the other end of the slough.

"The breeze is coming from the west, so let's paddle down to that end and then we can cast and float back across the lake," Ethan said.

"Good idea," Marshall agreed.

They paddled to the end of the lake and coasted to a stop. The slight breeze began moving them slowly down the lake. They each picked up a rod and reel and began casting to the weed beds and lily pads hoping to catch a bass or northern. Ethan had a strike on his second cast.

"Whoa, here we go!" he said with a wide grin.

"Dumb luck," Marshall said watching Ethan fight about a 6 pound northern.

Ethan brought the fish to the boat and grabbed it behind the head, lifted it into the boat and held it up. Buzz was very interested in the fish but he kept his distance since it looked kind of fierce with a mouth full of teeth.

"Pretty nice one eh?"

"Yeah, I guess."

Ethan grinned, took the lure from the fish's mouth and released it back into the water.

Buzz watched the fish disappear and then he stepped out over the side of the boat onto a lily pad. He went right to the bottom. Marshall gasped when he saw the dog disappear over the side.

"Buzzie!" he shouted. He jumped up from his seat and Ethan knelt in the bottom of the boat and they looked over the side. Buzz was on the bottom looking around like he couldn't figure out what was going on. The water was only a couple feet deep, so Ethan reached down and grabbed the little guy under the belly and lifted him up into the boat. Buzz looked at them and shook off and then climbed back up on the boat seat and settled down looking into the water again.

"He wasn't even afraid," Marshall said laughing.

"I guess he thought that lily pad was land," Ethan said. He picked up his rod and reel and cast to another clump of weeds. He'd only turned the reel handle two turns when he set the hook into another fish.

"Holy smokes, I've got another one!"

Marshall sat looking at his pal reeling in another fish and you could almost see the steam coming from his ears.

Ethan reeled in the fish and it was a twin to the other one.

"Another nice one," he said.

"Yeah, yeah, a couple of retarded northern... just dumb luck."

Ethan didn't say anything but let the fish go.

"What kind of bait are you using?" he asked.

"I've got a spinner on," Marshall replied.

"You should try a Miller Wobbler," Ethan said.

"This spinner is a killer, don't worry I'll catch up to you soon."

"Okay, suit yourself," Ethan replied.

This time it took five casts before Ethan hooked into the next fish. It was a nice largemouth bass.

"Well kiss my butt!" Marshall said.

Ethan burst out laughing as he lipped the fish and held it up. "What do you think?" he said holding the fish so Marshall could admire it. "Maybe you'd like to take a picture?"

"I think you need to lend me a Miller Wobbler," Marshall replied.

Ethan looked surprised. "What... you don't have a Miller Wobbler?"

"Obviously I don't have one or I'd have put it on my line by now."

Ethan was having a good time with this.

"Well, jeez, you tell me to kiss your butt and then you expect me to lend you a Miller Wobbler?"

Marshall sat there shaking his head. "Okay, I'm sorry, I didn't mean that," he said.

"And?"

If looks could kill the look Marshall had on his face would have slain Ethan right there.

"And, let me use one of your Miller Wobblers because I don't have any."

"I don't think I heard the word "please"."

Marshall took a deep breath.

"Ethan, would you please let me use one of your Miller Wobblers?"

Ethan smiled. "See, now that wasn't so hard was it?"

He dug in his tackle box and looked up. "It seems that I only have one left, do you promise to take good care of it?"

"You're lucky we're not hunting or I'd shoot you." Marshall said under his breath.

"Pardon me? What did you say?"

"I'll be very careful with it, I promise, and if I lose it I'll buy you another."

Ethan tossed the lure to the front of the boat.

Marshall couldn't get the lure tied onto his line fast enough. There was a nice clump of weeds coming up on the left and he wanted to be the first to cast to it. He reeled the lure up to the end of his pole, and cast hard to get to the weeds. The lure flew out across the water and his line went out faster than the reel spun and turned into a big snarled mess. When the gob of line got to the first guide on his pole it snagged up and snapped. The Miller Wobbler flew out across the lake and dropped into the water, unattached to Marshall's pole.

15

"What the?..."

Marshall sat there looking at the place where the last Miller Wobbler had dropped into the lake. He turned to look at Ethan and saw him lying in the bottom of the boat laughing so hard he had tears running down his face.

"Are you kidding me? Tell me you've got more of those baits," he said to Ethan.

Ethan shook his head. "That was the last one."

"Give me that one you've got."

"Bull crap. I told you to be careful with that one I gave you."

"Let's row over there. Maybe I can find it."

"Fat chance, it's gone, just try something else."

"I'm not going to sit here and watch you catch fish all day and not catch any."

"It's not the bait, it's the fisherman. I have massive skills," Ethan said.

"Oh baloney, help me paddle over there."

Ethan picked up his paddle and they rowed over to the spot the bait had disappeared. The water was clear as gin so they could see down into the weeds a long way.

"We'll never find it," Ethan said.

"Shut up, help me look," Marshall replied kneeling in the bottom of the boat and looking down into the water. Buzz came next to him and looked down too. Ethan moved them slowly around carefully with his paddle covering more area while Marshall watched for the lure. Suddenly Marshall yelled, "There it is!"

Ethan stopped the motion of the boat and moved up to where Marshall was kneeling. He looked over the side and sure enough, the lure was hanging on a weed about half way to the bottom. It was around five or six feet deep.

"It's too deep, you can't reach it," he said.

"I'm gonna try."

Marshall pushed the sleeve of his tee up and reached down into the chilly water. He went deep enough to get his sleeve wet but was too far away. He took off his shirt and tried again but was still short.

"Maybe I can get it with my toes," he said.

"Let it go, we'll get some more when we get home."

"No, I'm going to get this one and that's that!"

He took off his shorts and pulled his boxers up into his crotch so they'd stay dry and sat on the edge of the boat with his feet in the water. He let himself over the side as far as he dared and tried to grab the lure with his toes.

Ethan watched as Marshall gripped the lure between his big toe and the next one.

"You've got it!" he said.

Marshall began to pull his foot up and got almost to the top when the lure dropped from his grasp.

"Oh no!" he cried as the lure fluttered all the way to the bottom.

"Well, it's gone now," Ethan said.

"I'm getting that lure, and nothing's going to stop me," Marshall said.

He stood up, took off his boxers and slipped over the side of the boat buck-naked and into the lake. He gasped as the cold water engulfed him. Of course Buzz jumped in too since his master was going swimming, so was he. Ethan sat there looking amazed.

"Grab Buzzie," Marshall said.

Ethan coaxed the dog to him and pulled him into the boat.

"Here goes," he said. He took a deep breath and slipped under the water. Ethan watched as he swam to the bottom, grabbed the lure and came up to the surface. He tossed the lure into the boat and hung on the side gasping.

"Pull me up, I'm frozen."

Ethan grabbed Marshall's forearms and easily lifted him up and into the boat. Marshall was shivering but had a wide grin on his face.

"I gotta give you an A for effort," Ethan said. "I really didn't think you'd have the balls to do that."

Marshall looked down. "After being in that cold water you're correct, I don't."

They laughed for a long time after that. Marshall wiped as much water as he could from himself and then put on his clothes. It was a warm sunny day and it didn't take long for him to completely dry out.

He removed the snarl of line from his rod and tied the Miller Wobbler back on the end.

"Okay here goes," he said as he cast toward a beaver house. The lure landed, and Marshall began reeling it in toward the boat. As it came past a clump of weeds, the water swirled and a huge fish grabbed the lure. Marshall set the hook and the fight was on. The fish ran toward the middle of the lake and dogged down into the weeds. Marshall kept steady pressure on the line and soon the fish ran again and then came to the surface and jumped into the air.

"Holy crap, look at that one!" Ethan said. "That's got to be a 15 pound northern."

Ethan reeled up his line so he could help and watched as Marshall slowly worked the fish to the boat. It made several more runs but each time the run was shorter. Finally the fish came to the surface next to the boat and Ethan carefully grabbed it behind the head and lifted it in.

"Marshall, look at that, it's a monster."

Marshall was shaking with excitement. "Holy smokes, that's the biggest fish I've ever caught other than that paddlefish," he said.

Buzz looked at the fish and moved to the other end of the

boat.

The fish lay there, its gills working in the air. The boys sat admiring the beautiful critter.

"Let's put it back," Marshall said.

"Are you sure? It's a trophy."

"Yeah, let's let it live. It's been in this lake for a long time, I don't want to be the one to take it out and kill it."

Ethan smiled. "We don't have a camera, or even a ruler."

"Lay it on the paddle and we'll make a mark so we can see how long it was."

They lay the fish on the paddle, scratched a mark with another fishhook and Ethan lifted it up and put it into the water. He handed the tail end to Marshall.

"Work her back and forth to get some oxygen in her gills," he said.

Marshall pushed the fish back and forth and suddenly he felt strength return to the tail and the fish pulled away and disappeared into the lake depths. He sat there and looked into the water for a minute and then up at Ethan.

"That was a good thing," he said.

"Real good," Ethan added.

"Well, let's keep fishing," Marshall said. "But you know what?"

"What?"

"After seeing the teeth on that big thing, I'm going to think twice about going into the water naked again."

Ethan nearly fell out of the boat laughing.

They fished for a while and then loaded up and went home. After they'd put the boat away Ethan told Marshall to follow him up to his room.

"Look what I got," he said digging in his sock drawer. He pulled out a pack of 200 firecrackers.

"Holy smokes, where did you get those?" Marshall asked.

"One of the guys on the baseball team got them someplace in

Iowa. He was visiting his relatives and brought back a bunch of them for the guys on the team. I thought we'd take them along with us to Canada and have some fireworks back in the wilderness where we wouldn't get into trouble."

"Cool, that sounds like fun," Marshall said.

"Do you have any room in your tackle box?" Ethan asked.

"Yeah, I think I could fit them in, why don't you just pack them?"

"Oh I just thought it'd be better to keep them in a tackle box so we can blow some while we're out fishing. Plus they'll stay dry in a tackle box."

Marshall frowned but didn't see too much wrong with that logic.

"Sure I'll pack them in my tackle box. I've got one of those plastic lighters in there already."

"Good deal, we'll have fun with these I just know it," Ethan said, suppressing a grin.

16

The next few weeks went by quickly. The dads were hard at work getting everything done so they could take another week off to fish with their boys and the boys worked hard to get their final exams taken with good results. The school year was winding down and graduation was just a week away.

Ethan's mom was going frantic planning his party and the boys tried to stay out of the way. Even so they made countless trips to town for party supplies, food and many other items.

Marshall made a point to have his dad order a dozen Miller Wobblers for him from the store. They had a nice sporting goods department so Ethan and Marshall always had the best tackle money could buy... at wholesale prices.

Graduation was coming up on Saturday so Ethan was busy at school with practice and getting all signed out for the final time. Marshall was waiting for him when he got home carrying a bunch stuff from his locker and his cap and gown for the ceremony. He helped him carry the stuff upstairs to his room.

"So, tomorrow is the big day," he said.

"Yeah, I'm on my way out into the cruel world."

Marshall tried to smile but he was having a hard time. His eyes filled with tears and he turned away.

"Hey, it's ok Marsh, I'll still be here for you."

Marshall nodded but kept his back to Ethan.

Ethan walked up and put his arms around his younger buddy and hugged him. "No matter what, I'll be your friend, I promise," he said quietly.

Marshall nodded. "I know but it'll be different now. You'll go away and I'll still be here. And we'll see each other when you come home but it'll never be the same as it's been."

"Life goes on Marsh. We don't stay kids forever. Look at our dads. They've stayed friends for ages. I'm hoping that will be what we do too."

Marshall smiled. "Yeah, I didn't think about that. They've been friends for years, they'll probably be friends when they're old farts too."

Ethan laughed. "Don't let them hear you call them old farts. Now come on, Mom wants me to help set up chairs in the back yard and you're my helper."

The big day came and Marshall dressed in new khaki's and a nice blue button down shirt with a red and white striped tie. He wore "dress up" shoes for the first time in a year. He usually wore old cruddy tennis shoes or flip-flops in the summer so his feet were hurting within a few minutes of getting wedged into the hard shoes. He went with his parents to the school and they had passes so they got to sit in the special seating down front.

Soon everyone seemed to be in place and the band started playing Pomp and Circumstance. Everyone stood and the graduates began marching into the gym, two by two. Ethan was about half way back in the pack and was marching with his best friend from the baseball team. He looked handsome with his blond curls sticking out from under his mortarboard cap. When he got close to Marshall and his family he winked at his pal.

Marshall felt his heart in his throat. He was so proud of Ethan and so glad they were friends but he knew, from today on, things would change. He had a hard time keeping the tears back.

After what seemed like endless speeches and musical pieces by the band and chorus, the diplomas were handed out. Ethan's name was called and he strode across the stage, got his diploma and waved to his parents and Marshall's family. Then the band began playing Pomp and Circumstance again and they all marched out to the cafeteria.

It took nearly half an hour for everyone to file out to the cafeteria. Marshall stood on tiptoes and finally found Ethan standing in a line of other graduates shaking hands around the perimeter of the room. He made his way through the crowd and stopped in front of Ethan who was getting hugged by an aunt. They talked a minute and then Ethan noticed Marshall.

"Hey pal, what do you think?"

"I think you did good."

"How about a congratulations then?" Ethan said.

Marshall stepped up and held out his hand.

Ethan shook his head. "Nope that won't do."

He put his big strong arms around Marshall and hugged him hard. "You've made my life a lot of fun Marsh. If I had a brother I couldn't love him any more than I love you."

Marshall was crying like a baby. He stepped back and hurried away.

A while later at the party he shyly walked up to Ethan.

"I didn't mean to cry at school, but what you said really got to me," he said looking down at the ground.

"Marshall there's no reason to be embarrassed. All that we've been through together, makes us as close as brothers and I'm so glad I've always had you there."

"Even when I tied your toes together?"

Ethan grinned. "Even then."

Many hours later the party was over and everyone had gone home. Marshall's family helped clean up and then they went home, tired after a big day.

Marshall took off his clothes and was sitting in his boxers. He looked out the window and saw Ethan lying on his bed in some athletic shorts watching a baseball game on TV.

"No I shouldn't," he said to himself. He grinned, got up and got his remote. He waited for a long fly ball and then switched channels to Animal Planet. There was a hippo chasing a guy in a canoe and bellowing like mad. Ethan jumped up and grabbed his remote and changed the channel back.

"Damn TV!" he muttered.

Marshall put his remote down. "Once is enough for tonight," he said. Then he lay down and slept long and hard.

17

They loaded the vehicle the afternoon before their trip and had everything ready to go so they could leave early the next morning for Canada. After a cookout in Ethan's back yard everyone went home to get a good night's sleep.

Marshall lay awake for hours trying to sleep but the excitement of the fishing trip to the wilds of Canada had him so excited he just couldn't make it happen. He finally got up and sat on the edge of his bed. He yawned and scratched and happened to look across the gap between his bedroom and Ethan's and saw Ethan sitting on the bed scratching his head.

Marshall moved to the window. "Can't sleep?" he whispered loudly.

Ethan turned and looked and grinned. "Nope, too excited."

Marshall nodded. "How about some hot cocoa and a cookie?"

"You got some cookies?"

Marshall nodded. "I'll be over in a few minutes."

He went downstairs and heated some milk, added cocoa mix and stirred up two steaming cups. Then he slipped 4 oatmeal cookies in a bag and tiptoed through the house, across the wet grass and to Ethan's back door. Ethan was waiting for him carrying two blankets.

"Let's sit in the lounge chairs out here," he said.

Marshall put the cocoa and cookies on a little glass top table between two padded lounge chairs and sat in one while Ethan sat in the other. They each pulled a blanket across their laps.

"Umm, good," Ethan said.

"It's just a mix, but yeah, it's pretty good," Marshall replied.

They each bit into a cookie and both said "Mmmmm."

"Did you sleep at all?" Ethan asked.

Marshall shook his head. "Not a wink... all I could do is

think of flying into a lake later today. Have you ever flown in a plane?"

Ethan shook his head. "Nope, this will be the first time for me too."

"Are you a little scared?"

Ethan shrugged. "Not really scared, but a little tense I guess. These bush pilots are very good at what they do. Of course a lot of them crash every year. But I think we'll be fine."

"I guess we have to trust them."

Ethan nodded. "And hope they have years of experience."

They finished their cookies and cocoa and both sat back and pulled up their blanket to their chin.

"I told my dad that I've decided to go into the Marines when we get back," Ethan said.

Marshall looked at him. "Really? You're going to the Marines instead of college?"

Ethan nodded. "I just don't know what I want to do with my life. I figure I want to serve my country and after I'm done with the Marines I'll have a better idea of what I want to do next."

"What did your dad say?"

"He asked the same question but he was okay with it. I think he's proud that I'm going to serve. It's for 4 years, not forever."

Marshall felt like he had a stone in his chest. He sat quietly thinking that his time with Ethan was nearly over.

"Marsh, we'll still be friends. That'll never change. We just won't see each other every day."

"Yeah I know but it's hard to think of you being thousands of miles away."

"Oh, you've got other friends and pretty soon some girl will be stealing your heart and you'll forget all about me."

Marshall looked over at Ethan. "That will never happen Ethan... never."

Ethan reached over and took Marshall's hand in his and squeezed it. "That's good, we'll always be there for each other...

promise?"

"Promise."

They each lay back and in a few minutes they were both sleeping soundly. The sun was coming up over the back fence when their dads came out onto the patio and found them.

"Looks like the boys don't want to go to Canada," Marshall's dad said.

The boys woke and looked up.

"Holy smokes, what time is it?" Ethan said.

"It's time for you two to get a shower and meet us in the car. We're off on our great adventure as soon as you guys are dressed and ready to go."

It took Ethan 9 minutes and Marshall 11 minutes to shower, dress, and run to the car. Marshall took longer because he had to kiss Buzzie goodbye.

18

The boys were excited and everyone was talking about getting to the lake and going fishing. They stopped at a diner and had a big breakfast and then got back on the road. It didn't take long for both Ethan and Marshall to slide down in the back seat and fall asleep.

Time passed and the miles swept by and it seemed to the boys like they'd just fallen asleep when their dads woke them for lunch. They were on the highway that skirted Lake Superior and marveled at the huge lake as they pulled into a restaurant.

"Jeez, look at that thing, it's like an ocean," Marshall said.

"It's one of the largest freshwater lakes in the world," his dad said. "In fact it's over 31,000 square miles and holds 2,900 cubic miles of water."

Marshall just shook his head. "I hope the lake we're going to isn't that big."

"Nope, it's just a puddle compared to this one," his dad said.

"I guess we didn't tell you the name of the lake yet did we?" Ethan's dad asked.

"No, and I don't think we asked," Ethan said.

His dad grinned, "It's Marshall Lake," he said.

"No way!"

"Yeah, we thought that was pretty strange, taking you and Marshall to Marshall Lake."

Marshall grinned, "I'm gonna like this."

They ate lunch and filled up with gas and headed north. When they got to the city of International Falls the boys were pretty excited. They were going to another country.

They waited in a line of cars until they were at the border. A Canadian border guard came out and asked them their destination, if they were US citizens and the purpose of their visit.

"We're going to Marshall Lake, we're all US citizens and the purpose of our visit is for fishing," Marshall's dad said.

"Yeah, and my name is Marshall too," Marshall blurted from the back seat.

The guard looked into the back. "I see," then he turned to Marshall's dad who was driving. "Could you step out and open the back please?"

Marshall looked at Ethan and had a look of terror on his face. "Are they going to search us?" he whispered.

"Probably, we don't have anything we're not suppose to have... do we?"

"We've got those firecrackers in my tackle box."

Ethan turned to his dad, "Dad you might want to declare a few firecrackers."

His dad turned and looked into the back seat. "Oh, where would they be?"

"Marshall's tackle box."

His dad got out and walked back. They could hear him talking to the Border Guard. The guard opened the tackle box and took the firecrackers out. He said something to the dads and they got back into the car.

The guard came to Marshall's window and tapped on it. Marshall looked like he was ready to fill his pants. He rolled down the window.

"Is there anything else you want to declare young man?"

Marshall shook his head. "Umm, no sir."

The guard looked stern. "You know young man that you're now in Canada and not in the US."

"Yes sir."

"We are very strict on our smuggling laws and take them very seriously."

"Yes sir." Marshall's voice quivered and he looked like he might cry.

The rest of the guys were sitting looking straight ahead like they didn't know Marshall or want to be associated with him.

"I'm going to have to ask you to step out of the vehicle and accompany me to the office."

"What? I have to go with you?"

"Yes," the guard said. Then he reached into his pocket and pulled on a pair of rubber gloves.

Marshall looked at the others and they didn't turn or look at him.

"Dad?"

"You better go with the man Marshall."

He was shaking so badly he could hardly get out of the vehicle.

"What are the rubber gloves for sir?"

"We're going to have to ask you to strip and we have to do a body cavity search."

Marshall's mouth dropped open. "You what?"

He turned to his dad, "Dad... do something!"

His dad turned and had tears running down his face. Marshall looked and saw that Ethan's dad was laughing so hard he was crying and Ethan was lying on the seat choking from laughing.

"What?"

The Border Guard was also laughing now.

"You dirty shits!"

That made them laugh all the harder.

Then Marshall began laughing too.

"Ethan you turd, you set me up!"

Ethan wiped the tears from his eyes.

"I got you good this time little man."

The guard stripped off the rubber gloves.

"Have a nice time in Canada young man."

He turned and walked back to the Guard Station laughing.

Marshall got back into the vehicle.

"You guys are a laugh a minute," he said. "Just like a troop of freakin' circus clowns."

Marshall's dad turned in the seat and raised his eyebrows.

"Well, you must admit that was a classic."

"You were in on it all the time?"

"Ethan told us of his plan and I asked the guard to help. He was happy to prank you son. I explained that you love to prank people and he said he has a son just like you."

Marshall nodded. "I guess I had that coming. But you all better beware, this is war now."

His dad laughed and said, "Firecrackers aren't illegal in Canada, but they are in the US. If we'd been going the other way you'd have gotten us in trouble. This is a good lesson for you, and a good prank for the rest of us."

"Well, I'll be... " Marshall said.

"That was for the pudding," Ethan said wiping tears from his eyes.

Marshall sat back in his seat and grinned. That was a darn good prank. Now he'd really have to work to top that one.

They drove on north and a little over 4 hours later they pulled into the office and landing for the outfitter they were using for their trip. There were two planes tied up at the dock. One was much larger than the other but both were painted in sky blue paint with yellow trim.

"Are those the planes that we fly in?" Marshall asked.

"Yeah, that smaller one is called a Dehavilland Beaver and the bigger one is a Dehavilland Otter. We'll be taking the Otter," his dad said.

"Cool, is this the one you took the last time you were up here?"

His dad nodded. "Yeah, it's a nice little plane."

Just then a kid not much older than Ethan came out of the little log cabin office. He was tall and skinny with long blond hair tied back in a ponytail. He was wearing a sleeveless blue tee shirt, cutoff jeans and hiking boots. He walked up to them.

"Hello, you must be our fishermen that are going to Marshall Lake eh?"

Ethan nodded. "Is your dad here?"

The kid looked quizzically at him.

"My dad? Why would he be here eh?"

"We're flying in," Marshall said, "doesn't he fly the plane?"

"My dad's a dentist. He's in town, the boss is inside but I fly the plane."

Marshall looked at his dad. He grinned.

"Marshall, Ethan, this is Derrick, he's our pilot."

"Really" Ethan said. "How old are you?"

Derrick grinned. "I'm 20, been flying for almost 4 years now."

"No kidding? Wow," Ethan said.

Derrick turned to the dads, "How about you go in and get the paperwork done with Phil and me and the boys will load the plane?"

The dads agreed and walked into the office.

"So, are you guys brothers?" he asked.

"No, just best friends," Ethan said, "But we're as close as brothers."

"Good deal, well, let's get your gear loaded and then we can take off. I've got her all gassed up and we're ready to fly."

"So you really can fly that thing?" Marshall said.

"Yeah, I really can. I haven't had a crash in over three weeks."

Marshall looked at him.

"Just joking eh?"

They started carrying the gear down the dock and Derrick got into the plane and took the stuff and stowed it as they handed it in to him. When everything was stowed away he tied a cargo net over it all and they closed the cargo door.

"Ok, here comes your dads, so we can take off," Derrick said. "Who wants to sit up front with me?"

Marshall's eyes got big. "You go," Ethan said.

"Really you don't mind?"

"I'll sit there on the way back at the end of the trip," he said.

They all climbed onboard the plane and Derrick instructed Marshall to untie the ropes that held the back and front of the plane to the dock.

He got the plane started and once it was running, he shouted to Marshall to push the front away from the dock and jump aboard. Marshall did as he was told and once inside he buckled his seat belt. His heart was hammering in his chest partly from excitement and partly from pushing the heavy plane away from the dock.

"Ok, everybody belted?" Derrick asked over his shoulder.

There was a chorus of "yes" so he throttled up the plane and they began moving down the lake away from the wind.

"We'll take off toward the west tonight," he said loudly to Marshall. "We want to go into the wind."

Marshall nodded.

The lake was a little choppy with small waves slapping against the pontoons. They taxied down to the east end of the lake and Derrick turned the plane around using the tail rudder. He checked his gauges and wiggled his eyebrows. "Ok," he said, "here we go!"

The engine sped up and the sound turned into a roar as they began moving down the lake. Marshall was hanging onto the seat arm and watching the water fly past. They went faster and faster and soon Marshall noticed an orange milk jug floating up ahead of them.

"What's that orange jug for?" he shouted.

"We have to be off the water by there or we'll hit the trees on the island," Derrick said without turning toward him.

Marshall watched the jug get closer and closer. Soon it was only fifty feet away and they were closing on it very fast.

"Are we gonna go up?" he asked.

"I hope so eh?"

They got to the milk jug and kept going. "You better stop!" Marshall shouted.

He closed his eyes as the shoreline got closer and closer.

Suddenly the banging of he water against the pontoons stopped and they soared into the air missing the trees by twenty feet. The plane went up at a very sharp angle with the engine screaming.

Marshall opened his eyes and took a breath. He looked over at Derrick who was laughing.

"What the heck?"

"Sorry, your dad asked me to do that," he said. "It does add a little to the excitement doesn't it?"

Marshall turned in his seat and saw his dad and Ethan and his dad laughing.

"This is war," he said.

They laughed all the harder.

Soon they were a thousand feet in the air flying over millions of pine trees, swamps and lakes. Marshall looked out ahead of them and it looked the same for miles and miles.

"Do you ever see any bears or stuff?" he asked.

Derrick nodded. "Sometimes," he said.

They flew for about 40 minutes and Marshall was enjoying the ride. Suddenly the plane tipped on the side toward him and dove sharply toward the ground. He grabbed the seat and pressed his feet to the floor. "What? What?"

Derrick pointed. "There's a moose down there eh?"

Marshall looked out the window and sure enough there was a moose standing in a little pond of water.

"Great, thanks for showing me that," he said. "Do you want to go back up and find my stomach?"

Derrick righted the plane and they flew on with a grin on his face.

"Oh Derrick?" Marshall said.

"Yeah?"

"I don't need to see any more wildlife. And by the way, do you have a place on here where I can change my underwear?"

Derrick laughed and laughed and on they flew.

20

Ten minutes later Derrick pointed ahead, "That's Marshall Lake eh?"

Marshall looked and could see a large lake on the horizon. He turned and looked into the back of the plane and Ethan was grinning.

"That's it," he said pointing.

Ethan nodded that he understood.

"We might still have time to fish," he said loudly.

Marshall nodded enthusiastically.

They flew on and when they got close to the lake Derrick put the plane into a dive that almost made Marshall's butt come off the seat. He banked to the left and circled the end of the lake and dropped almost to the water.

Marshall was hanging on for dear life and watched as Derrick flew toward a dock sticking out from the bank, slowed the speed of the plane and dropped onto the water like a leaf falling from a tree. They bumped across some small waves and when they got within about a hundred yards of the dock, Derrick killed the motor and opened his door and jumped out onto the pontoon. The plane coasted up to the dock and Derrick jumped onto it with the bow rope in his hand and wrapped it around a post sticking up and the plane stopped. The tail end slid toward the dock when the nose stopped and Derrick was already at the rear end pulling the rope tight and tying it to another post.

"Here we are," he said smiling widely.

"Jeez, it looks like you've done that a few times," Ethan said from the back.

"Just a few," Derrick said.

Marshall got out onto the dock and the others did the same. Meanwhile Derrick opened the cargo door and began setting their gear onto the dock. They all picked up a bag or box and carried everything up to the cabin.

The boys stopped and looked at the cabin. They were kind of surprised but the dads had already been there so they just walked ahead with Derrick.

"Jeez, talk about the basics," Ethan said.

"No kidding, we had a fort in the back yard when we were about ten that was as good at this," Marshall said shaking his head.

The cabin was not much more than a place to get in from the rain. The floor was built up on two-foot tall 4x4s and the walls were plywood. There were five 4 x 8 sheets on each side and four sheets on the ends. The front had two windows cut into it and the end had a porch and a door. The roof was corrugated tin.

They walked up the steps and into the single room. The studs were bare and the rafters also were bare. You could see the plywood on the outside walls and the tin on the roof. In the middle of the room was a 55gallon oil drum that had been made into a wood stove. Against the back wall were a refrigerator and a stove and a sink. There was a table and 4 chairs and four single bunk beds. Two gas lanterns hung from two rafters.

"Just like home eh?" Derrick said grinning.

"Just like," Marshall said.

The dads laughed. "We're here to fish, not to sit inside," his dad said.

"Yeah, I guess you're right. Um, where is the toilet?"

Derrick motioned for him to come with him. He and Ethan followed him down a trail back into the woods. They walked for nearly 40 yards and there was a "two-holer" sitting complete with quarter moon slits in the doors.

"Here she is," Derrick said.

Ethan opened the door and looked surprised. "Two holes?" he said.

Derrick shrugged. "In case you want company."

"Why is it so far away?" Marshall asked.

"Well, stick your head in and take a whiff," Derrick said. "Also it's best to keep it away from the cabin in case a bear comes along and finds it."

"Are there bears here?" Marshall asked excitedly.

"Of course," Derrick said. "A big one came right into the camp last week. The guys cleaned their fish and left the guts on the dock instead of taking them out and dumping them in the lake. Two of them were sitting down on the dock having a beer later that evening and a big old bear walked right up behind them and carried off the bucket of guts."

"Holy smokes." Marshall said.

"Bears will leave you alone but moose, you're better to stay far away from them."

"Really? Are they dangerous?" Ethan asked.

"They get a bit cranky sometimes. I'd advise you to leave them alone. They look big and slow but believe me they can run pretty dang fast."

Marshall grinned. "It sounds like you speak from experience."

Derrick nodded. "Me and a buddy were fishing one day and just drifting and casting and we drifted right up on a big old bull. Never saw him because we were looking the wrong way. All of a sudden we heard a "Mmmmuuuuu!" We turned around and he was about three feet from our canoe. He started for us and by the time we grabbed our paddles he'd gotten one front foot into the canoe and almost tipped us over. We paddled like our lives were lost and managed to get away with just a big dent in the canoe and wet clothes. My buddy crapped his pants too," he said laughing. "I never let him forget it either."

"We'll be careful," Ethan said.

They walked back to the cabin and the dads came out.

"Well, you guys know how to run everything so I guess I'll get out of here," Derrick said.

"Remember if you need help, put a white tee shirt on the

dock."

"That's how we get help?" Marshall asked.

"That's it eh. We fly to other camps every day and always fly over ones with fishermen in them. If I see a white tee shirt, I'll drop in and see what's up."

They all thanked Derrick for his good driving and he untied the plane and pushed it off from the dock. When it was away a bit he started it and drove it out into the lake. He turned and began takeoff across the water gaining speed and suddenly he lifted off the water and into the sky. He banked over them and wiggled the wings and they watched as he disappeared over the trees.

"He's quite a guy," Ethan said.

"You guys were kind of surprised to see such a young pilot, weren't you?" Ethan's dad asked.

"Yeah, he's not much older than I am, and look at me I'm a baseball player and he flies planes."

"Your time will come," his dad said.

"Let's go fishing," Marshall said.

"You guys go, we'll get the cabin all shaped up. Here, look," Marshall's dad said pointing down the lake. "See that eagle's nest on the shore over there?"

Ethan and Marshall looked and saw it.

"Go past it to the left a little way and you'll see a little stream that runs into the lake. Drop some jigs and twister tails down there and jig them and you'll have walleyes in no time. Bring back half a dozen or so for supper."

Marshall smiled. "Just like that? Go catch our supper?"

His dad nodded. "Just like that."

21

E than and Marshall took one of the 25HP motors out of the little cabinet on the dock and also grabbed a gas can. They selected one of the identical Lund boats lying upside down on the dock and lifted it into the water. They tied a rope from each end of the boat to the dock so it stayed put while they loaded up. Marshall handed Ethan the motor and he clamped it onto the back of the boat and hooked up the gas line.

"Ok," Ethan said, "Hand me our fishing stuff and we'll go and see what we can catch."

Their gear was still piled on the dock so Marshall sorted his and Ethan's stuff out and handed it to him in the boat. When everything was loaded he untied the front of the boat and Ethan untied the back and they pushed off. Ethan pulled the starter chord three times before the motor came to life. Then he put it in Forward and off they went across the lake.

There was a little chop on the water; the air temperature was in the low 70s. Marshall sat looking forward and felt exhilarated as the wind blew through his hair. He turned and grinned at Ethan. His cheeks had a red tinge like they usually did when Ethan was happy.

"Pretty dang great," he said.

Ethan smiled and nodded. "I wonder what our friends are doing today?"

They headed across the lake toward the eagles nest. When they got close Ethan slowed down and Marshall saw the creek coming into the lagoon. He pointed and Ethan took them over near the creek. He shut off the motor.

"Well, here we are," Ethan said.

"I'll bet you a nickel I catch the first fish," Marshall said.

"You're on."

They both hurried to put their rods together and string their line. Ethan had a jig tied onto his line first and he put a twister tail on the jig and cast out. Marshall was just half a minute behind him.

Marshall lifted his rod and raised the jig, letting it fall back to the bottom. He lifted it a second time and felt a tic on his line. He knew that was the tic of a walleye inhaling his jig so he set the hook.

He turned to Ethan to give him the news that he had the first fish on but was surprised to see Ethan fighting a fish already.

"What? How did you catch that so quick?"

"You gotta know how to wiggle your jig," Ethan said boating a nice walleye.

Marshall fought his fish and half a minute later boated a twin to Ethan's fish.

"Well, that sucks," he said.

"I'll let the nickel ride and when we get home you can pay up. I expect many more nickels will be coming my way before we finish the trip."

"Don't count on it," Marshall mumbled.

The next fish came a few casts later and they fished for about a half hour and had 8 walleye that were perfect eating size.

"We should head back, that's enough for supper," Ethan said.

"Do you think our dads have everything carried up and put away?" Marshall asked.

Ethan grinned. "Maybe we should take our time going back."

They started the motor and drove the boat along the shoreline looking for more prospective fishing spots. Every time they saw a creek running into the lake they tried to keep a mental picture of where it was. About half way back they came to a large bay full of lily pads. Ethan slowed and then stopped.

"This looks like a northern hot spot," he said.

"No kidding, all these weeds, they should be full of big northern."

"Did you bring your Miller Wobblers?"

Marshall grinned. "I have 20 of them."

Ethan laughed. "Well I have a dozen. We won't run out."

They got back to the dock and their dads were sitting on lawn chairs waiting for them. They were having a cold beer.

"So do we have supper or are we going to have bologna sandwiches," Ethan's dad asked.

Marshall lifted up the stringer and they grinned.

"Walleye it is," his dad said.

There was a cleaning bench on the dock.

Ethan's dad explained that they should clean the fish and put the heads and guts in a bucket that was on the dock, and then take it out and dump the guts in the lake. There were plastic tubs also on the dock to bring the fish up to the cabin.

The boys said they'd do as instructed so the dad's went up to start on some potatoes and beans to go along with the fish.

"Where do we get water to wash them off?" Ethan asked.

His dad nodded toward the lake. "That's where we wash, bathe and get our cooking water."

It didn't take long and the fish were ready to be fried. Marshall picked up the gut pail and asked Ethan if he could take them out and dump them.

"Are you sure you can run the boat?"

"You did it, I don't know why I can't do it."

Ethan shrugged. "Okay, see you up at the cabin."

He walked up a little way and turned and watched Marshall take off from the dock. At first he was a little hesitant but soon he opened up the motor and was flying out toward the middle of the lake. Ethan watched as Marshall slowed down and stopped and then dumped the pail. Then he took a big circle and started back. About half way back he made three big circles, jumping over his wakes. When he pulled up to the dock he had a giant grin on his face.

"Man, this is the coolest," he said as he got up on the bank where Ethan was waiting.

"This'll be a trip we'll never forget," Ethan said.

22

While Marshall and Ethan had been gone the dads boiled some potatoes and filled the wood box in the cabin for a fire later when the air cooled down. They had everything ready for the fillets and in no time the cabin smelled like a Friday Night Fish Fry at their favorite local restaurant. The boys stowed their gear in a couple of wooden dressers and laid out their sleeping bags on two of the bunks and by the time they were finished, so was the supper.

They all sat and ate fried walleye fillets, fried potatoes and warmed-up beans until they couldn't eat another bite.

"Oh man, I think I'm about to explode," Marshall said.

The boys cleaned the dishes and pans and they went out and sat on the porch of the cabin and watched the dusk turn to dark.

"I don't know about anyone else," Ethan's dad said, "but I'm ready for bed. Today started a long time ago."

They all agreed and while the dads were settling into bed Marshall and Ethan walked a little way away and peed into the bushes.

"What if one of us has to poop during the night?" Marshall asked.

"I guess he has to walk back to the little toilet in the woods," Ethan replied.

"Jeez, in the dark?"

"There's a flashlight sitting on top of the refrigerator for that I think," Ethan said.

Marshall nodded. "I hope I don't have to."

The boys stripped down to their underwear and got into their sleeping bags and everyone settled down for the night.

Marshall lay in his bed thinking of the amazing things he'd done and seen that day and was smiling as he drifted off to sleep.

It was very dark when he next opened his eyes. He wondered what had awakened him and lay there listening. Soon he heard a noise coming from the countertop by the sink. There was a crunching and rattling sound that must have woke him up. He sat up and looked trying to see what was making the noise but it was too dark.

Finally he couldn't stand it anymore so he got out of his sleeping bag and tiptoed over to the counter. There was something rattling around in the grocery box. He felt the top of the refrigerator and found the flashlight. Then he turned it on and shined it into the box.

There were about half a dozen mice scurrying around and they'd eaten a hole in their bag of un-popped popcorn. Marshall grabbed the closest thing he could see to use as a club and slammed it down on one of the mice.

"Bang!"

"What the heck?" his dad said from his bunk. "Marshall what the heck are you doing?"

Bang! "I'm killing mice. They're carrying off all of our popcorn."

By now everyone was awake and they watched Marshall hammer mice with a skillet. It didn't take long and he had flattened every one of the mice.

"I got seven of the little buggers," he said.

"Good work," Ethan's dad said. "Put the rest of the popcorn into the refrigerator and we'll take care of it in the morning."

Marshall closed up the bag and stuck it in the refrigerator and sprinted back to his bunk.

"Nice job killer," Ethan said from below him.

"Thanks. Just trying to do my part," he said.

It didn't take long for everyone to go back to sleep. The next thing he knew he smelled bacon frying and looked across the room to the kitchen area. Ethan was in a tee shirt and shorts, tending a pan of bacon while his dad was making toast with a little device that sat over a burner on the stove.

"Where's dad?" he asked.

"Up in the privy," Ethan said.

"I gotta do that too," he said and jumped down from the bed. He slipped on his shorts and flip-flops and hurried back to the outhouse. He met his dad on the way.

"Everything come out ok?" he asked grinning.

"You bet, those beans were a good stimulus for me," his dad said.

"See you in a bit," said Marshall as he hurried to the little house.

He dropped his pants and sat there. He'd never been in a true outhouse like this and it was kind of cool. There were some hunting magazines piled up on the seat next to him and he picked one up and paged through it while he did his business.

When he came into the cabin the breakfast was ready and they all ate like they'd been starved.

"So who's fishing with who today?" Ethan asked.

"We thought each dad would fish with his son and that way we can show you guys all the good spots we found last time we were here. Then from today on we can pair up as we choose. That sounded good to the boys so after they cleaned up the breakfast mess they went down to the dock and rigged up a second boat.

The dads came down to the dock and they loaded up and soon they were going down the lake throwing a nice wake behind the boat. They all headed to the east end and fished several places catching walleye, northern, and some huge perch. Then they trolled some rocky shorelines for lake trout. The morning slipped past quickly.

"Let's catch half a dozen walleye and have shore lunch," Ethan's dad called from the other boat. They pulled up where a little creek came into the lake that had a big beaver house in the bay next to the creek. In no time they had six walleye in the boat.

The dads had brought a box that held a couple of frying pans, some boiled potatoes and a can of beans and some oil.

They pulled up on a big flat rock shelf and put the anchors on the shore to keep the boats from floating away. Ethan walked up into the woods and came back with some firewood and they started a fire. Marshall found four rocks the same size and set them in a square and then they set a little metal grate over the rocks.

The boys took the fish down by the water and filleted them while the dads got the potatoes and beans cooking. In no time they had the fish fried and were eating fish, potatoes and beans.

"Oh man," Marshall said as he ate.

"Pretty cool eh?" Ethan said.

"Yeah eh?"

They all laughed. "This is the life," his dad said.

"We should plan to do this every year from now on," Ethan's dad added.

"It's a deal, every year from now on, we'll come up here fishing," Marshall said.

They all toasted the plan.

23

That night they played poker after the evening meal. It had cooled off so Ethan made a fire in the stove and the cabin was warm and cozy.

They talked about many things as they played. The subject of Ethan joining the Marines finally came up and his dad said he was very proud of him.

"While I'm a little apprehensive about the possibility of your getting hurt or even killed, I couldn't be prouder that you're going to serve," he said.

"What do you want to do in the Marines," Marshall's dad asked.

"I'm going to look into being a dog handler. I saw a film and read a book about those military dogs and they're amazing animals. I think it would be something to be one of their handlers."

"So are they like attack dogs?" Marshall asked.

"Some are, but most are bomb detection dogs," Ethan said.

"Really? You want to find bombs?

"It's not as dangerous as it sounds," Ethan said. "These dogs can detect .025 grams of explosives. That's like a grain of sand. With a dog like that by my side I'd probably be safer than most of the others out there. These things are highly trained and I think it would be really great to work with them."

"Well, I know Buzzy is highly trained," Marshall said. "He can detect an M&M in my pocket from three feet away."

They all laughed at his goofy remark.

"All we want is for you to do your best and keep your head down," Ethan's dad said.

"And come home in one piece," Marshall added.

"I promise," Ethan said.

They all went out to pee and then undressed and climbed into their bunks. During the night it stormed and the rain clattered on the roof but by morning it was clear and sunny. They ate breakfast and walked down to the dock.

"I think we're going to try trolling for some Lake trout," Ethan's dad said.

Ethan looked at Marshall. "What do you think?"

"I'd rather catch some northern," he said.

"Well then we'll meet you on that same rock for lunch," his dad said.

"We'll bring some 'lunch fish'."

They took off in different directions and soon Ethan and Marshall were throwing spoons and spinners along a weed bed that bordered a small river that ran into the lake. Marshall was having a field day catching northern after northern on his Miller Wobblers. Ethan was using a spinner-bait and doing equally well.

"This kind of spoils you for fishing when we get back home," he said as he fought a nice fish.

"Yeah, it sure does."

They fished on and Marshall had a hit on his bait that seemed like a little fish. He reeled it in and found a four-inch perch that was impaled on the hook.

"Look at this, I hooked this little guy in the tail," he said.

"Put him out for bait," Ethan said.

"Hey, good idea," Marshall said.

He picked up an extra rod and tied a leader on it and put a large hook on the leader. Then he snapped a big red and white bobber on the line about four feet up from the hook and put the hook in the tail of the perch. He reeled up the slack and threw it out toward the middle of the lake.

"Maybe a huge one will grab it," he said nodding.

"Maybe."

They fished on and half an hour later Marshall farted. He giggled about it and clenched up to fart again but stopped with a worried look on his face.

"Oops, that's not a fart," he said. "Take me over to the shore... quick."

Ethan laughed. "Hang your butt over the side and go."

"No way, hurry up I gotta urgent call to nature!"

Ethan fired up the motor and took him to shore. He pulled up next to a big rock and Marshall jumped out onto it and ran for the woods. Ethan picked up Marshall's extra rod and reeled in the perch. Then he took an empty soda can and hooked the hook through the pull-tab and held it over the side and filled it with water. He reeled it up and cast it out to the middle. When the soda can hit, it went right to the bottom and took Marshall's bobber with it.

Pretty soon Marshall came back through the brush.

"I thought maybe a bear ate you," Ethan said.

"Whoo, if he smelled what came out of me, he would have run away. By the way willows make terrible toilet paper."

Ethan laughed. "Get in, we've got fish to catch."

Marshall jumped in and Ethan backed up the boat. Marshall noticed his extra rod lying on the bottom of the boat and looked out toward the lake.

"Hey, where's my bobber?"

Ethan looked. "I don't know, maybe a fish grabbed that perch while you were otherwise detained."

Marshall picked up the rod and reeled slowly trying to feel resistance. Soon he got the slack reeled up.

"I feel something," he whispered.

"Is it moving?"

He nodded.

"Should I set the hook?"

Ethan nodded.

Marshall slammed the hook into the "fish" and began reeling. The pop can rolled over the bottom and spun as it was being reeled in and it caused a lot of commotion.

"It feels like a big one," Marshall said playing the "fish".

Ethan could barely keep a straight face.

"I'll get the net ready," he said. He picked up the net and laid it on the edge of the boat. Then he got his camera ready.

"I'll get an action shot," he said.

"Boy this is the trophy of the day," Marshall said excitedly.

Ethan nodded. "Looks like it."

Marshall worked the "fish" in close and when he started to raise it from the bottom he warned Ethan that it was coming up.

"Get ready I'm winching him up!"

Ethan leaned over the side and got his camera ready and when the pop can came out of the water he took a picture of it and of Marshall's surprised face.

"What the?"

Marshall swung the can aboard and looked over at Ethan who was nearly falling out of the boat laughing.

"You must have hooked that can, what a great fisherman to do something like that," he gasped. "It takes a real master angler to get his hook in that little pull tab."

Marshall grinned and took the can from his line and swung it at Ethan slopping all of the water over him.

"You'll pay," he said. "You will definitely pay."

24

"So here's a picture of Marshall catching a keeper Soda Trout," Ethan said handing his dad his camera. The dads were laughing as they looked at the surprised look on Marshall's face.

"I've never caught one of those," his dad said. "I had one on once but it broke my line." There was uproarious laughter.

Marshall just nodded. "Keep it up, you'll all pay."

That evening they walked down to the dock at dusk and sat and watched the darkness envelope the lake. There was a firepot for roasting marshmallows and weenies on the dock so they made a fire and sat and talked about the fishing and whatever came up.

"So have you looked into the Marines?" Marshall's dad asked Ethan.

"I talked to the recruiter when they were at the school a few weeks ago," Ethan said.

"So you're pretty sure of this?"

"Yeah, I just don't know for sure what I want to do with my life. I've thought of a few things that interest me but I don't think I'm ready to commit to something yet," Ethan said. "This way I have a few years before I have to decide."

"Well a commitment to the Marines is a quite a commitment," his dad said.

"I know that and I'm ready for it. I think I'm in pretty good shape and can learn almost anything. I know there's a war going on but I'm prepared to do my part. The odds of getting hurt or killed are in my favor. I know some guys get hurt but most don't get hurt. I hope to be one of those."

"You just keep your head down and don't do something stupid," Marshall said.

Ethan smiled at his younger buddy. "Don't worry Marshall, I'll come back and we'll grow old together just like our dads."

"Whom are you calling old?" his dad said.

"You know what I mean," he said.

"I'm hungry. I think I'll go up and pop some popcorn," Marshall announced. "Everyone want some?"

There was a chorus of "yes".

Marshall was hungry but he also had an idea. When he got to the cabin he opened the cupboard and grabbed the box that held the mousetraps that had been left there. He set nine traps and then carefully unzipped each of the others sleeping bags and lay three traps in each bag near the bottom. He zipped up the bags and then went and fired up a big pot and made a couple of batches of popcorn. He dumped it into two big bowls and returned to the dock.

Everyone was glad to dig into the popcorn and an hour later they were yawning and ready for bed. They walked up to the cabin and everyone took turns brushing their teeth and doing their bathroom duties.

"Go ahead and get in your sleeping bags," Marshall said. "I'll put the lantern out when everyone is ready."

He couldn't keep the grin off his face. Ethan was the first one to slide into this bag. He let out a yelp and then another as two of the traps snapped on his feet. The dads were just seconds behind him and Ethan's dad ended up with one trap on his toe and another on his calf. Marshall's dad managed to get all three traps on one foot.

In no time they were all out of their sleeping bags yelling and hopping around on one foot or pulling traps off their toes. Ethan looked at Marshall and shook his head. '

"You little turd," he said.

The dads had the traps off their feet and were laughing.

"You know what this means Marshall," his dad said.

"No what?" Marshall said laughing crazily. "Oh wait, I know, there are no mouses in your sleeping bags?"

"It means war," his dad said.

"Ooooo, I'm all shaking in my shoes," Marshall said giggling.

"Shut the light off, wise-guy."

Marshall giggled and grinned for a long time before he went to sleep. He was surprised when dawn came so fast. He could smell bacon frying and woke to see his dad and Ethan making breakfast.

"You guys are walking pretty good," he said.

"Don't be a smart butt," Ethan said. "My little toe is damaged."

Marshall burst out laughing. "Damaged?"

Ethan grinned. "Shut up and make some toast."

"I gotta poop first," Marshall said. "It's an emergency."

He jumped out of bed and slipped his shoes on and ran out the door. He hustled as fast as he could up to the outhouse, opened the door and sat on the right side hole. As he sat there he heard a thump sound from outside. He listened but no more sound came so he didn't think much about it. When he was finished he fastened his pants and pushed on the door to leave. The door wouldn't open. He pushed harder but it was shut tight.

"Those dirty shits," he thought to himself.

He put his shoulder to the door and pushed and it didn't budge. "Hmm."

He looked up and around the inside of the little house and there was no other way out. And the worst part was that is was pretty aromatic in the place. Years of use gave the thing a smell that was strong to say the least.

"Okay, very funny," he said.

"Come on, let me out now, you've had your fun."

There was no sound from outside.

Inside the cabin the other three were laughing and grinning as they ate breakfast.

"What do you think? Should we let him out?" Ethan said.

"Let's go fishing for a while and let him stew."

"Really?" Ethan asked.

"Marshall is the prankster of pranksters. This will be a good lesson for him."

They cleaned up the cabin and walked down to the dock. They all three got into one boat and cast off. Ethan's dad was driving and he pulled on the starter cord, got the motor going and off they went.

Marshall heard the outboard start. "They're going to make me think they left me behind," he thought to himself grinning.

He waited a few minutes expecting to hear the log or whatever was blocking the door being removed.

"Okay, I know you're out there," he said through the wall.

"Come on guys, enough is enough, it stinks like hell in here."

"Dad?"

"Hello?"

25

Marshall knew he was going to be in the outhouse for a while when half an hour had passed. There was no sound from outside and he finally resigned himself that they'd left him behind. There was a pile of old newspapers on the seat and he searched through them and started reading. Most of the papers were years old but at least it gave him something to do to pass the time.

"Those guys are going to pay for this," he said to himself.

He was hungry. He'd missed breakfast and it must be nearly lunchtime. He smiled when he heard the sound of an outboard coming up the lake. He listened and it sounded like it came to the dock and shut down. Soon he heard footsteps on the path outside the outhouse.

"Hey let me out," he shouted.

"Marshall? Marshall where are you?"

"I'm in the outhouse as if you didn't know," he said.

"How did you get in there? How did this log get against the door?"

It was Ethan and Marshall could hear the laughter in his voice.

"Could you please remove the log?"

"Sure, glad to buddy."

He heard the log scraping against the door and then Ethan opened it and stepped back. "Holy cow, we wondered where you'd gone. It looks like this log fell off one of these trees and just happened to land against the door of the outhouse. What a coincidence."

Marshall could hardly keep from applauding Ethan's performance.

"So you just decided to go fishing and left me behind?"

"Funny you should ask. We thought you might have taken a boat and gone fishing by yourself, so we went looking for you."

"Oh was there a boat missing?"

"You know, we didn't count boats. I guess we were pretty worried so we just missed that clue."

Ethan was having a hard time keeping a straight face. He looked up into the trees.

"What a strange thing. What do you suppose the odds are of a log falling from a tree and land against the door?"

"You will pay," Marshall said as he stomped past Ethan.

He could hear Ethan giggling behind him as he walked up to the cabin. The dads were inside preparing lunch.

"Well there he is. What were you doing? Bird watching?"

"You two are real comedians. Add Ethan to your team and you could be like the Three Stooges."

The dads tried to keep a straight face.

As they ate Marshall cooled off.

"Marshall I think you should go down to the lake and take a bath. You smell a lot like the inside of the outhouse," Ethan said.

Marshall just glared at him.

"Or not," Ethan said.

"We were thinking we should go out on a father and son fishing trip this afternoon," his dad suggested.

That sounded good to the boys, so after they put away the lunch fixings they walked down to the dock and paired up with their fathers. The agreed that each boat would bring in 4 fish for dinner.

Marshall and his dad pulled up in front of a creek mouth and started drifting across the bay, jigging for walleye.

"Dad, what do you really think about Ethan going in the Marines?"

"His dad and I talked about it. Ethan doesn't know for sure what he wants to do with his life. He also wants to do something for his country. His dad is very proud of him but of course he's a little worried about him too."

"What do you think?"

"Ethan is a very smart kid and will be successful at whatever he does. He's certainly tough enough for the Marines and I think he'll do well. We'll all have to pray for him to keep him safe."

"I don't know what I'm going to do without him," Marshall said.

"You guys are as close as brothers," his dad said.

"It's going to be really strange not having him there every day," Marshall replied.

"Well, you'll get used to it. Ethan will be home eventually and you guys can keep in touch with emails and stuff. It's not forever."

"Yeah, I suppose." Marshall felt an empty feeling inside him and he knew it would be even worse when Ethan left. It was something he wasn't looking forward to.

They fished for another hour and had four nice walleye on the stringer. The sky was turning dark and the wind was coming up.

"Looks like we're going to get some nasty weather," his dad said.

"Let's head in and clean these fish."

They were just a hundred yards from the dock when Ethan and his dad came around an island and headed toward them. They got to the dock about the same time and unloaded the boats.

"You guys pull the boats up on the dock and take the gear out and then take the motor off and put it in the storage box. Then turn the boats over on top of the gear. That way the gear will be dry and the boats won't be full of water tomorrow."

Ethan and Marshall did as they were told while the dads went to the fish hut and cleaned the fish. The boys were just passing when the dads came out. It was just starting to rain and the wind was blowing quite hard.

"Leave the guts on the dock," Ethan's dad said. "There's no hurry to take them out in this weather."

"We'll start dinner and you boys carry in a bunch of firewood. It might rain for a day or more and we'll want some dry wood."

By the time they had the wood stowed in the cabin the dads had the dinner ready. They ate and talked about many different things. After the dinner was cleaned up they played Monopoly for a couple of hours. The wind howled and the rain hammered against the windows.

"Getting pretty darn nasty," Ethan said.

"It's not fit for man nor beast," Marshall added.

"This old man is ready for bed," Ethan's dad said yawning.

"I gotta poop first," Marshall said.

"I'm glad it's you," Ethan said, "I sure as heck don't want to go out in that rain."

"If I don't I'll lay awake all night thinking about it," Marshall said.

He put on his poncho and grabbed a flashlight. "If I'm not back in fifteen minutes, you'll know a bear ate me." He walked out into the night.

Just as soon as Marshall stepped off the porch the wind blew his hood off and the rain beat down getting his hair all wet. He pulled the hood up and hustled up the path to the outhouse.

"Why in the heck did they have to put this thing half a mile away?" he said to himself.

He made it to the outhouse and shut the door, leaving the flashlight on and laying on the adjacent seat. He did his business and started back down the path.

"I'll probably get pneumonia," he grumbled as he slogged along on the muddy path.

He was nearly to the porch when he heard, "Huff".

He stopped and raised the flashlight up off the path and shined it around. About five yards away on the path from the dock he saw eyes shining in the light. "Huff!"

"Holy crap!" he whispered.

He ran as fast as he could to the porch. The ground was slick with mud. As he turned the corner to go up the steps his feet slid out from under him and he went down on his butt. He heard a crashing and cracking through the brush.

He jumped to his feet and slipped and slid up the steps. He was shaking badly as he grabbed the doorknob. His hands were covered with mud and they slipped around the knob. The hair was standing up on his neck as he tried to get the door open.

"I'm going to be eaten alive," was going through his mind.

Finally the door opened and he ran inside. His feet went out from under him and he slid onto his rear end on the floor. The door slammed shut when his head hit against it.

The other three were already in their beds and they all sat up.

"Marshall, what the heck are you doing?"

"A bear! A huge freaking bear!"

"A bear, where was it?"

"It was chasing me."

"It chased you?" his dad asked.

"Well, not really chased. It was more like it was on the other path."

He hesitated. "Now that I think about it I think it was running the other way."

There was silence. Then all three of them began laughing.

"It's not funny!"

They laughed harder.

"Are you sure it was a bear? Maybe it was a large raccoon?" Ethan said.

"Oh you guys are just a laugh a minute. You're just like Comedy Central."

The others were still laughing when Marshall dried himself off. His shorts and underwear were all wet from falling in the mud and he had to put on dry boxers. He got into his bed still shaking.

26

They only had two days left at the lake. Marshall and Ethan wanted to fish for northern with their Miller Wobblers and the dads wanted to try for lake trout so they went one way toward the deep end of the lake and the boys went up to the other end to fish weed-beds for northern.

"Let me drive," Marshall said as they put their lunch into the boat.

Ethan looked at him and then shrugged. "I guess you know as much about it as I do," he said. "Just try to steer us away from those huge rocks," he said.

"Duh, I wouldn't have thought of that," Marshall said.

They took off down the lake and Marshall loved the fun of driving the boat. The motor was only 25HP but it pushed the 16 foot V bottom boat right along. They stopped at a bay that was full of weeds and lily pads and he shut down the motor. The wind was coming from across the lake so they just let the boat drift through the pads and began casting.

It didn't take long for Ethan to get a hit and he fought about a 5 pound northern to the boat. He took his Wobbler from its jaw and released it and just at the same second Marshall set the hook into a twin.

"Boy this is the way to do it," he said as he fought the fish. He got it to the boat and grabbed it behind the head, lifted it into the boat and pulled his bait from its jaw. He grinned as he released the fish.

"This has been a really cool week," Ethan said.

"Yeah, we've had a lot of fun," Marshall replied.

"You know, a lot of kids dad's wouldn't take the time to do this or a lot of kid's don't have a dad to do with at all."

"We're really lucky we've both got great dads," Marshall said.

Just then Ethan hooked into a much larger fish.

"Oh boy, this is a big one," he said as his drag screamed from his reel. Marshall reeled in his line and sat and watched as Ethan fought the fish. The water boiled as he worked it next to the boat and then the fish took off and gained almost all of the line that Ethan had reeled in. The next time it got close Marshall saw it flash next to the boat.

"Holy crap Ethan, it's a huge one!"

Ethan worked the fish and soon it came from the water and jumped. "Wow, that's a 20-pounder," he said.

Ethan fought the fish for another 5 minutes and finally it was tired out enough that he could grab it behind the head and drag it into the boat. It lay on the bottom it's mouth opening and closing and it's gills working.

"A monster," Marshall said looking open-mouthed at the fish. "Jeez that's the biggest northern I've ever seen."

He got his camera from his tackle box and Ethan held up the fish. Marshall took several pictures of it and then Ethan lifted it over the side and let it slip back under the weeds.

"What a fish," Ethan said.

"That made the whole trip worthwhile," Marshall said. "Now I gotta catch one like that."

They'd drifted into the end of the bay but Marshall turned and threw his lure back out toward the deeper water.

"I'm going to re-tie my lure," Ethan said. "Those northern have sharp gill plates and I'd hate to take a chance on nicks and cuts in my line and lose the next one plus lose my Miller Wobbler."

Marshall nodded and kept casting toward the middle of the bay. Ethan was sitting in the bow seat facing backward toward Marshall and took his clipper and cut the lure off and then cut off about 5 feet of line. Then he began to tie the lure back on the end of his line.

Marshall turned around to see if he was done so they could

move the boat back out into the bay and his mouth dropped open. About ten feet behind Ethan stood a huge bull moose eating a mouthful of aquatic weeds.

"Holy crap," he whispered.

Ethan didn't look up. "What's wrong?" he said as he finished up tying the lure on.

"Behind you."

Ethan looked confused. He turned around and his eyes got real big when he looked up at the moose towering over the boat, now only 6 feet away.

"Back us up!" he said desperately.

The moose looked down at Ethan and it seemed as it he'd just noticed them. He "huffed" and then bent his head down. "Muuuuuuuuuh!"

Ethan was up and stumbling back toward the back of the boat.

"Marshal, get the motor running!"

Marshall grabbed the starter cord and pulled. The motor sputtered but didn't catch. He pulled again and it started.

By now the moose was acting more and more angry. It came forward and was less than a foot from the bow of the boat.

"Back us up... hurry!" Ethan said almost climbing onto Marshall's seat.

Marshall put the motor into reverse but it didn't go very well because the weeds were very thick and the prop was full of them.

"We're stuck!" he said urgently.

"Turn us, real tight!"

Marshall reached around and put the shift lever into forward, turned the motor as hard to the right as he could and gunned it. The boat spun to the left and smacked into the moose's chest as it passed by. The moose bellowed and stepped back. They went past it and in seconds were several feet away. The moose was now very angry and took off through the water chasing them. They made better time than it did and in a few more seconds they were safe.

For good measure Marshall took them a hundred yards out into the bay before he shut the motor off. Ethan was sitting on the floor of the boat at Marshall's feet looking up at him.

"Did you do that on purpose?" he asked.

"What? I was fishing. I didn't see that thing. You were the one who was in the front, why didn't you see it?"

"I was busy. I heard something splash back there but thought it was a beaver or something."

Marshall looked down at Ethan sitting on the bottom of the boat. Here was the guy he's hero-worshipped his whole life, sitting looking like he'd just peed his pants.

"Did you pee yourself?" Marshall said grinning.

Ethan smiled widely. "No, but I came close. Boy that was a surprise. That damn thing was huge, especially from where I was sitting on that front seat."

"Get up you look like a sissy sitting there," Marshall said.

Ethan punched him in the leg and got up. He moved to the front of the boat.

"Well that's one that we'll remember for a long time," he said.

"Want to keep fishing?" Marshall asked.

Ethan nodded. "Just keep us a little way farther from shore from now on."

They laughed and began fishing again.

27

"So Ethan screams like a 12 year old girl and comes running to the back of the boat crying. He laid on the deck of the boat with his arms over his head and I think he peed himself," Marshall said to the dads who were laughing so hard they had tears running down their faces.

"He's yelling, Marshall, Marshall, save me!"

Ethan grinned and looked at his friend.

"Laugh it up," he said. "One of these days…"

They were sitting around the table in the cabin finishing up a walleye dinner. They had just one day left of their vacation and tomorrow didn't look good weather-wise. The wind was coming up and it had just started raining so fishing in the morning was not a sure thing.

"If the weather is okay tomorrow one of you guys better take Ethan, he's too much trouble for me."

They all laughed again and Ethan got up and grabbed Marshall around the head and gave him a noogie.

They cleaned up the dinner mess and played Monopoly until everyone began yawning. Marshall and his dad walked out on the porch to water the bushes and hurried back because it was raining pretty hard.

"Doesn't look good for fishing tomorrow," his dad said.

Marshall shrugged. "I'd like to get one more day in but if it gets too nasty, I guess we can play Monopoly."

It DID get nasty. All night the wind rose and the rain came harder. By morning the whole lake was covered in fog and the wind was whipping through the trees. They spent the day packing up and eating as much food as they could so they didn't waste anything. By evening they were all ready to head home.

"What time is Derrick coming in the morning?" Ethan asked.

"He said to be ready any time between 9am and noon. He has to pick up parties of fishermen from several other lakes too.

Then once he gets them all back, he'll start taking the new groups out to the lakes. He'll be a busy young man."

The wind was still very strong and gusty the next morning. The rain had stopped and the fog had been blown away. They carried their clothes and gear down to the dock and pulled the boats up and turned them over. They put the motors into the cabinet on the dock and then went back up to the cabin to get out of the cold wind.

At a little past 9 o'clock they heard the plane coming toward the lake. They closed the door and latched it tight and walked down to the dock. Derrick came from the south, which was over he cabin and circled the lake. He was flying the smaller plane. When he got past the trees on the other side he dropped down and lost altitude to land. The plane was whipping back and forth and the wings looked out of control as he fought the wind. Finally he got close enough to the lee side, near them and he dropped onto the lake. The pontoons splashed and dipped deep into the water and it looked like the plane was going to tip over on its nose. But Derrick kept control and taxied into the dock.

"A bit bumpy eh?" he said.

"A lot bumpy, is it safe to fly?" Ethan's dad asked.

"I'm going to take two of you back and then come for the other two. That way I can take off near this shore where it's not so rough. If I take all of you I'll be too heavy with all the gear and have to start over on the other side where it's so rough. It'll take forty five minutes to go and then come back."

"We'll stay," Ethan said. "You guys go back and get the vehicle ready. Then when we get back all we have to do is throw our stuff in."

The dads agreed that was a good idea. They loaded their gear into the plane and got in with Derrick.

"Be back in a jiffy," Derrick said.

He fired up the plane and taxied out onto the lake. He stayed closer to the shore near the cabin and went down the lake a way until he had enough room for a takeoff. The boys watched as the prop began to spin faster and faster and the plane skimmed across the waves toward the lee end of the lake. There was a lot of splash from the waves hitting the pontoons but suddenly the plane lifted off the water and up it went. Derrick pulled into a steep climb and just missed the trees on the end of the lake. When he got out of the shelter of the trees the wind whipped the plane around like a balsa wood toy but he soon stabilized it and disappeared out over the forest.

"That looked pretty exciting," Marshall said.

"I'll bet our dads about pooped," Ethan laughed.

"Don't make jokes, we have to take that ride too," Marshall said nodding his head.

"Well we might as well spend the waiting time up in the cabin where we'll be out of the wind," Ethan said starting for the cabin.

"Yeah, there's no sense in standing here freezing to death."

They walked up to the cabin and went inside.

"Did you see that the music department at school is going to do the play *Les Miserables* next fall?" Ethan asked.

"Yeah I saw a poster."

"Why don't you try out for it?"

"Me? I can't sing that well."

"Baloney Marshall. You sing better than me. Remember quite a few years ago our parents took us to that play?"

Marshall looked confused.

"I don't remember for sure. How long ago was it?"

"I think I was 7 or 8 so you probably were only 6. I guess you might not remember it. It's a story about the French Revolution and peasants who revolt. The music is really good."

"Okay, I remember something like that. But why would I want to be in it?"

"The play needs a lot of guys. Many of the main characters are men and boys. There are quite a few good singers in the choir now and I think that's why they want to do this play. If you try out and get a part it will give you something to keep you busy when I leave for the Marines. And you'll meet some new people to hang out with."

"So when are you leaving?" Marshall asked.

"I'm leaving for basic training in about a month. Then I'll be gone for three months and if I get into the Military Dog program I'll be gone another four months."

"You already know that? Why didn't you tell me?"

"I didn't want you to worry about it."

"You'll be gone for almost a year?"

Ethan nodded. "But then I'll come home and have a leave and then I don't know for sure."

Marshall sat and looked down at the floor.

"Hey Marsh, it's not forever. I'll be home someday and in the mean time we can email and Skype."

"I know but it won't be the same," Marshall said quietly. "I can't think of one day when I didn't see you or do something with you. We've been together our whole lives."

Ethan got up and sat next to Marshall on the bed where he was sitting. He put his arm around the younger boy.

"Marsh, we're growing up. We're both becoming adults. It'd be nice to be kids forever but that doesn't happen. No matter what we'll always be best friends... that'll never change."

Marshall's eyes filled with tears. He hugged Ethan and buried his face in his chest. "I'm sorry I don't mean to be such a baby," he choked.

"It's fine. Don't worry we'll always be there for each other... no matter what."

Marshall nodded. "Okay then." He wiped the tears from his eyes. "You don't have to tell anyone about me crying okay?"

Ethan nodded. "As long as you forget about me and the moose," he said.

Marshall grinned. "Deal."

28

The wind seemed to be blowing even stronger as they sat in the cold cabin and waited. Finally Marshall laid back on one of the beds and drifted off to sleep. Ethan was thinking about leaving home in a short time when he heard the whine of the plane's engine.

"Hey, wake up, Derrick is back," he said.

Marshall opened his eyes and yawned. He got up and they walked to the door. They walked out on the porch and Ethan latched the main door and then hooked the screen and they jogged down to the lake.

Derrick was circling the lake and coming in to land from the other side, into the wind. The wings on the plane were wobbling back and forth and once it seemed like the whole thing was going over on its side.

"That looks pretty scary," Marshall said as he watched the plane touch down and the pontoons began splashing into the waves.

"I'm sure Derrick wouldn't be flying if he didn't think he could handle it," Ethan replied.

As the plane got closer to the dock they could tell that the waves were smaller the closer Derrick got to them. They were in the sheltered part of the lake where the wind was bad but not as bad as it would have been on the other side.

Derrick taxied up to the dock and the boys each grabbed one of the ropes attached to cleats and tied them to a hook on each end of the right pontoon. Derrick shut the plane down and climbed out onto the dock.

"Whew, it's getting pretty windy," he said.

"Is it okay for us to fly?" Marshall asked.

"I think we're okay. We better get going though because the forecast is for the wind to get even worse in the next couple of hours. I want to be back at the lodge by then."

The boys handed Derrick their luggage and fishing tackle and he stowed it in the back of the plane.

"Who is riding shotgun?" he asked.

Marshall turned to Ethan. "You go ahead, I sat in front on the way into the lake."

Ethan nodded and Marshall climbed into the back part of the plane and strapped in. Ethan let Derrick get in and start the plane and then he untied first the rear rope and then the front rope and pushed off from the dock as he stepped onto the pontoon and then up into the right seat. He cinched his seatbelt tight and looked over his shoulder at Marshall. Marshall flashed him a thumbs-up and grinned.

"Okay, here we go," Derrick said.

He taxied the plane out into the lake and soon the wind caught them and took them across and to the east end. The plane shook and rocked back and forth as the wind gusts hit it. They just drifted along until Derrick decided they were far enough for a good take-off. Then he taxied them as close to the lee shore as he dared go and they started for the windy end of the lake.

The pontoons were crashing into the waves and making a lot of racket as they increased their speed. Derrick was concentrating on the instruments and speed indicators.

"Are we okay?" Marshall shouted from the back.

"It's a bit touchy but I think we're good," he answered.

The speed increased and they were moving quickly toward the north shore. Derrick pulled back on the yoke and the plane lifted off the water. It immediately became much quieter without the noise from the pontoons. He pulled back hard and the plane went up at an extreme angle.

Ethan felt his stomach clench up as they were pushed back in their seats by the G forces of the plane accelerating at such a hard angle. They came up from the relatively calm air at the surface to the strong winds just at the treetops. The plane tipped to the left and Derrick struggled to right it.

"Hang on!" he said urgently.

Ethan grabbed the armrest on his seat and looked over his shoulder at Marshall. He was pale and looking scared.

The plane righted and then quickly was buffeted again and went over on the left side so drastically that all they could see out of the left window was water. Derrick struggled to right the craft again and managed to come nearly to upright when one of the pontoons slammed into a pine tree on the shoreline. The plane jerked almost completely around backward and flipped over.

"Derrick!" Ethan yelled. He knew they were doomed so he leaned forward and put his head down between his knees. He covered his head with his forearms and waited for the impact.

Derrick was doing all he could but they were upside down and going too slow to remain aloft. It seemed like minutes passed but it was really only a few seconds and the plane slammed into the lake nose first.

The prop was still spinning many thousand revolutions per minute and made a huge splash as it hit the water. The plane hit so hard it was almost completely submerged. Ethan looked out his window and all he could see was water.

The plane was still sealed up and was like a big bobber so it quickly popped to the surface. The problem was that it was upside down. The engine stopped and Ethan looked over at Derrick. He was slumped forward and his head was bleeding badly. Ethan grabbed Derrick and yelled at him. He reached out and turned his face and knew immediately that their pilot was dead. Derrick's blue eyes stared at him unseeing.

Everything was upside down and very disorienting. Ethan was hanging from his seatbelt. He quickly turned to the back and saw that Marshall was unconscious. He turned to his seatbelt and then he realized that water was pouring into the interior of the plane. By the time he got his seatbelt off the water level was half way up into the cabin. He dropped to what had been the roof of the plane.

"Oh God, we're going to the bottom," he thought to himself. He looked over at Derrick again just to be sure and he could see blood pouring from a gash in his head. The blood was spreading out through the water. He knew there was no help for Derrick.

"I've got to get to Marshall," he thought.

29

The plane was now nearly full of water. Ethan got his head up near the top and took a deep breath and then pushed himself into the back of the plane. Marshall was still hanging upside down and was completely under water. Ethan grabbed furiously for his seatbelt and it snapped free easily. Marshall dropped free of his seat and Ethan grabbed his limp body. He was running out of air so he surfaced to get another breath. There were only a few inches of open air at the top of the space. He took one more deep breath knowing it would be his last. He had to get Marshall out of the plane or they'd both drown.

He wrapped one arm around Marshall and grabbed the latch on the side door of the plane. It moved and he slid the door open. He pushed off the seat with his feet and he and Marshall slipped out into the lake. He fought for the surface holding onto Marshall with one arm.

When he came to the surface he gasped and gulped in a big breath of air. He looked around and they were fifty yards from shore and moving away toward the middle of the lake with the wind blowing across the water.

He looked at Marshall and knew he wasn't breathing.

"I gotta get him breathing before I try for shore," he said to himself.

He turned and saw the pontoons floating upside down on the water and swam for the closest one. He pushed as hard as he could and got Marshall up onto the pontoon. Then he hauled himself out and turned Marshall over so he could do CPR. He did several compressions on his heart and then gave him two breaths. He waited a few seconds and repeated the procedure. The wind was howling and the waves were getting larger as they moved closer to the middle of the lake. The water was freezing.

"Come on Marshall, come on and breathe," he yelled.

The cold water was sapping his strength. He wanted to climb out on the pontoon and rest but he knew he had to keep trying to bring Marshall back or he'd die.

"I can't quit," he said to himself with determination.

He kept working on his pal and suddenly Marshall vomited up a huge amount of water and began coughing.

"That's it! Keep on breathing, keep it up!"

Marshall was still unconscious but he was breathing. Ethan looked around and tried to figure out what to do. They were now at least a hundred yards from the shore where the cabin was.

"If we drift all the way across the lake we'll freeze," he thought to himself. "I've got to get Marshall indoors and get him warmed up."

The longer he waited, the farther the plane drifted out into the lake and the farther they were getting from safety, so he slipped Marshall off the pontoon and then put his arm around his chest and began swimming toward the shore.

The waves were slamming into him and he was getting colder and colder. He'd made about half the distance and was getting terribly tired.

"I can't rest, I have to keep going," he thought. "If I don't Marshall will die and I might too."

As tired as he was he kept swimming. The closer he got to the shore, the less the wind hit and the smaller the waves were. Soon he was swimming in almost calm water. He made much better time then and soon he was near the shore. He checked the water depth and he could stand up so he carried Marshall up onto the rocky shore and laid him down. He collapsed and lay there panting with exhaustion.

"I can't rest, I need to get him warmed up," he said out loud.

Ethan looked down the shore and saw the dock about fifty yards farther down along the waterline. He checked Marshall's breathing and he was doing fine, so he picked him up and carried him along the shore. It took several minutes until he could see the cabin through the brush. Then he cut directly through the woods to the cabin.

He carried Marshall up onto the porch and laid him down. He opened the screen door and then the main door, picked him back up and carried him inside. He laid Marshall on the floor next to the stove, closed the door and then stopped to think what to do first. He looked down at his friend and his lips were blue with the cold. His breathing was very shallow. Ethan knew he was suffering from hypothermia.

"I've got to get him warmed up," he said.

They were both soaking wet so he pulled Marshall's shoes and socks off, stripped off his jeans and underwear and then his jacket and shirt. He went to the steel trunk where they'd stored the pillows and blankets that stayed with the cabin. They were in a steel trunk so the mice wouldn't chew them all to pieces between fishing parties in the cabin. He took out a heavy blanket and laid it on the bed. Then he picked up Marshall and laid him on the blanket and rolled it up around him.

"I'll make a fire," he said. He was shivering and staggering from exhaustion but knew he had to keep going to get the fire going.

Thankfully they'd left a half full wood box when they left earlier. There was dry wood and kindling so it didn't take long to get a fire crackling in the stove. He filled it as full as he could so the cabin would warm up quickly. Then he stripped off his wet clothes and wrapped himself in another blanket.

He checked Marshall and he looked like hell. His face was white as a sheet and his teeth were chattering. His breathing was very shallow.

"He's not warming up," he thought to himself. "There's only one thing to do and I hope he keeps sleeping or he'll have a shit fit."

Ethan unwrapped Marshall's blanket and lay down next to him and then wrapped both blankets around the two of them. The only way to get Marshall's body warmed up was to put his body next to him and that was what he was going to do."

Exhaustion took over and in a few minutes Ethan was sound asleep. In his dream he saw Derrick floating in the water, blood coming from the wound in his head. He could hear him calling to him... "Ethan, Ethan."

30

than shook himself awake. At first he didn't know where he was but then he remembered the plane crash and Marshall drowning. He looked at his friend and Marshall was looking at him.

"What happened?" Marshall said weakly.

"We crashed the plane," Ethan replied.

Marshall digested that for a minute. "Where is Derrick?"

Ethan shook his head. "He died Marshall. He hit his head and was dead when we hit the water."

"Oh no," Marshall said with his eyes filling with tears. "I don't remember getting out of the plane."

"You were knocked out."

"Did you get me out?"

Ethan nodded.

Marshall coughed and clutched his chest. "My lungs feel funny, like I can't get a good breath."

"You had a lot of water in your lungs Marsh," Ethan said.

"What do you mean?"

"Well you weren't breathing, I had to do CPR on you but I got you started again and swam with you to the shore."

"I was dead?"

Ethan shrugged. "You were unconscious and not breathing. I guess you might have been but not for very long."

"So you saved my life?"

"I guess, I just did what I needed to do to keep you with me. I wasn't going to quit on you."

Marshall blinked back tears. "Thank you," he said.

"No problem," Ethan said smiling.

Then suddenly Marshall got a questioning look on his face. "Am I naked?"

Ethan nodded.

Marshall thought for a minute. "Are you naked too?"

Ethan grinned. "Yes I am."

"Holy crap, why are you and I naked and in the same blanket?"

"Calm down. We were both hypothermic. The water was very cold and we were in it for a long time. I made a fire but the only way to get warmed up quickly was to share body heat, so I stripped you and then I did the same and wrapped us up together. It's not like I was trying to cuddle you."

Marshall giggled. "Let's not tell anybody about this though."

Ethan nodded. "I think we're warm enough." He pulled the blankets back and gave one to Marshall and took one for himself. They each wrapped up in their blanket.

"We need to wring out our clothes and then hang them close to the fire to get them dry," he said.

They gathered up the clothes and took them out onto the porch. They each wrapped their blanket around their waist like a huge bath towel and each took an end of each piece of clothing and twisted to get some of the water out. Then they took the clothes and draped them over chairs near the stove, which was heating like crazy. They sat their sneakers near the stove on a stool and then sat down on the bed next to each other.

"Do you remember anything?" Ethan asked.

"I remember thinking Derrick was having a hard time getting us up high enough. I don't remember much after that. Are you sure he was dead?"

Ethan nodded. "He hit something hard with his head. I looked into his eyes and I knew. We were lucky that both of us didn't get knocked out or we'd be dead too."

"What are we going to do now?"

"We'll have to wait. When we don't return they'll send out another plane. I wish we could contact our dads. They'll be worried sick."

Marshall began coughing again. "Dang my chest hurts," he

said clenching his chest with his forearms.

"Let me see," Ethan said.

Marshall opened his blanket and Ethan looked at his chest. There was a big bruise on the left side just below his nipple.

"Do you remember hitting anything?"

Marshall thought. "It's foggy but now that you mention it I might have hit my chest on the other seat. We were kind of upside down?"

Ethan nodded. "Yeah, you're remembering more. We flipped over. You might have some broken ribs. Jeez, I might have done that when I was pushing on your chest."

Marshall began coughing again. "Well I'd rather have broken ribs than be dead," he said smiling.

Ethan put his arm around his pal. "I'm glad you're okay Marshall, I don't know what I'd do if I lost you."

"Thanks for saving me Ethan. I'll never forget it."

They both lay down wrapped in their blankets and soon they were both sleeping.

31

E than woke to the sound of Marshall coughing. He looked over at his pal and was shocked at how pale Marshall's face looked. He put his hand on his forehead and it felt very hot.

Marshall opened his eyes. "Is the plane here?" he said weakly.

"No, I woke up because you were coughing badly. How do you feel?"

"My chest hurts. When I try to take a deep breath I can't get enough air into my lungs. My head aches like crazy too."

Ethan got up and checked the clothes. They were dry. He grabbed his and dressed and then he helped Marshall get dressed. Their shoes were still wet so they just wore their socks.

"I'm starving," Marshall said.

"Me too."

Ethan looked out the window. It was still overcast and windy.

"There's no way to tell what time it is, but I'd guess it's getting late in the afternoon. I bet they'll wait until the wind dies down to come and get us."

"I bet our dads are worried sick. They have no way of knowing that we crashed."

Ethan nodded. "They must be going crazy with worry."

He checked the kitchen cabinets for any leftover food. Most groups of fishermen left some stuff behind for the next group. If things were there for more than a day without people being in the cabin, the mice got into them and they were ruined. So consequently they left things in the refrigerator.

Ethan opened the fridge and smiled.

"Well, we have a jar of un-popped popcorn, two sticks of butter, and a tomato."

Then he opened the cupboard and found some tea bags and

a jar of sugar. There was also a sleeve of Ritz crackers that hadn't been chewed into yet.

"Boy that sounds good to me," Marshall said.

Ethan grabbed a pan and a lid. He melted some butter in the pan and poured in some popcorn. He put it on the stove and began to shake it. Marshall stood up but bent over in pain.

"Lay back down and rest. I can take care of this," Ethan said.

"Okay I'm not gonna argue," he said.

"I'll run down to the lake and get a pail of water for some tea," Ethan said.

He grabbed the water pail from the counter and sprinted down to the dock. The rain had nearly stopped but the wind was still howling. He knelt on the dock and dipped the pail into the lake and filled it. As he stood up he looked out across the water. There near the other side he could see the pontoons next to shore with waves breaking over them. He shuddered as he thought of Derrick's body still in the plane. But it wouldn't do any good to go and try to retrieve it, so he turned and ran back up to the cabin.

It smelled like a movie theater inside the cabin. Ethan filled the coffee pot with water and set it on the stove. Then he put a couple more logs in to build the fire.

"How's it look outside?" Marshall asked.

"Still really windy, it's almost dark, they won't come tonight," Ethan replied.

He made a second batch of popcorn and dumped it into the big stainless steel bowl that he'd put the first one in. Then he melted some butter on it and salted it.

"Well at least we have something to eat," Marshall said. Then he began coughing hard. He bent over in pain.

"That doesn't sound good," Ethan said.

"It feels worse," Marshall said clutching his side. "My lungs feel like they're on fire and when I cough my ribs hurt really bad."

The water was hot so Ethan made two coffee mugs of tea and they sat on the edge of the bed and ate their popcorn.

"Well it's not much but it's filling," Ethan said.

"Tastes pretty good to me," Marshall said.

When they finished they sat and just talked for a while and then decided the time would pass faster if they tried to sleep. They both went out and did their business in the bushes and then climbed into the bed and both covered up with the two blankets they'd wrapped themselves in earlier. It felt good to have someone close like that when they were stranded out in the middle of the wilderness.

"I wonder if Derrick has any brothers and sisters?" Marshall said.

"We don't know anything about him do we? Of course we only spent a few hours with him. Even so he was a cool guy. It's sad to see someone so young have to die like that."

"Yeah, it is. But he died doing something he loved. I know he loved flying, you could see it in his eyes when we were up there."

Ethan nodded. "Well, get some sleep buddy."

Marshall rolled over and hugged Ethan tight. "Thanks again for saving me."

"Any day Marshall, any day."

He put his arm around Marshall's chest and gently held him as they fell asleep.

32

During the night Ethan slept fitfully as Marshall coughed more and more. His breathing became labored and he sounded congested. Ethan got up during the night and piled more wood on the fire as the cabin cooled down. Then finally he was tired enough that he slept soundly until dawn.

"Ethan?"

Ethan opened his eyes and tried to focus. At first he didn't know where he was and then he remembered the plane crash.

"Ethan, I feel awful," Marshall croaked. Then he began a wracking cough that shook the whole bed.

Ethan got up on one elbow and looked down at his young friend. Marshall looked terrible. His face was very pale and around his eyes the skin was sunken and dark, like zombie makeup at Halloween. He put his hand on Marshall's forehead and it was very hot. Marshall began coughing again and Ethan sat him up to keep him from choking.

"I feel like crap," Marshall whispered.

"You're sick, you've got a bad fever. You might have pneumonia too."

"My chest hurts really bad."

Ethan knew he didn't have anything in the cabin that would help Marshall so he got a glass of water and tried to get him to drink some. Marshall swallowed a little and then began coughing heavily.

"Lay back and stay warm," Ethan said. "I'm going down to the lake and see how it looks."

Marshall nodded.

The shoes were now dry so Ethan put his on and walked down the path to the dock. The lake was flat and there were just a few ripples on the surface from a slight breeze. The sky was mostly blue with a few fluffy white clouds here and there. He could still see the pontoons floating on the other side and shuddered thinking that Derrick's body was still strapped in the pilot's seat.

Suddenly he turned his head and could hear the sound of a plane coming from the south. He watched the sky as the sound of the engine got louder and then the plane appeared over the southwest end of the lake. He began waving when he saw it and the pilot waggled the wings letting him know he'd been seen. He watched as the plane circled the lake and then dropped to the surface. The pontoons made a double wake as they plowed through the water toward the dock. Ethan could see the pilot and another person in the front and when they got closer he saw it was his dad. Then he saw a face from the back seat and knew it was Marshall's dad.

He waved at them and he could see the wide smiles on their faces as they approached the dock. He grabbed the front rope and tied it to the front of the plane and as he ran to the back to tie it up, Marshall's dad jumped out of the back door and ran to him.

"Where's Marshall?" he asked looking very worried.

"He's up in the cabin. He's sick, but he's alive."

By then the engine had stopped and the other two were on the dock. Ethan's dad hugged him and said, "We were so worried. But the wind was so bad we couldn't get them to come to look for you."

"We spent the night in the cabin," Ethan said.

The pilot stepped up to him. "Is Derrick in the cabin?"

Ethan shook his head.

"No I'm very sorry, Derrick was killed when we crashed. His head was all bashed in and he was dead before we even got water in the plane. We hit a tree with a pontoon and the wind spun us around and we hit the water upside down. I was lucky enough to have my head shielded by my forearms but Derrick stuck to the controls trying to right us."

The man's eyes filled with tears.

"Derrick is my grandson," he said. Then he turned and walked to the other end of the dock. They let him alone in his grief.

"You said Marshall is sick," his dad said, "what's wrong with him?"

"He says his chest hurts so he might have a broken rib or two, and his lungs were full of water, and I think he might have pneumonia. His breathing is getting worse all the time and he has a bad fever."

"His lungs were full? Was he breathing?"

Ethan shook his head. "When I got him out of the plane he wasn't breathing. I did some chest compressions and gave him some breaths and he came back. I might be responsible for his broken ribs. I was kind of excited and may have pushed too hard."

Marshall's dad hugged Ethan. "Thank you for saving him. I don't know what I'd have done if we'd have lost him."

"We need to get him to a doctor," Ethan said.

The pilot got the plane ready for them to board and the dads and Ethan went up to the cabin to get Marshall.

They walked up to the bed and he opened his eyes. He looked like death warmed over.

"Hi dad," he said weakly. "We crashed."

His dad nodded. "Ethan told me all about it Marshall. We need to get you to a hospital."

Marshall nodded. "I feel like shit."

His dad grinned. "You look pretty much like shit too."

Marshall looked up at his dad and then broke into a wide smile.

"Don't let mom hear you talk like that."

His dad picked him up and carried him down to the dock. Ethan and his dad gathered up the rest of the stuff from the cabin and locked it up again. They followed down to the dock. Marshall was already strapped into a seat and his dad was right beside him. Ethan got in the back seat and his dad took the copilot seat after he'd taken the ropes off the plane. The pilot started the engine and took them out to the middle of the lake.

He looked at the pontoons floating on the surface near the far shore. "We'll come back for him," he said sadly.

They taxied down the lake and soon they turned and he pushed the power to full and they flew down the lake until they were going fast enough. They lifted off the lake and turned south, toward the closest hospital.

33

When they were safely in the air Marshall's dad put his arm around his son and Marshall laid his head on his dad's chest and fell asleep.

"He's not well," Ethan said.

"He needs a doctor quickly," his dad said.

The pilot called ahead on the radio and requested that an ambulance be waiting for them when they arrived at the outfitter's camp. A bit later he received a call that the ambulance was on its way.

They flew over miles of trees and dozens of lakes and soon they saw the base camp with all of the docks and another plane sitting on the water. They circled and landed on the lake and then were met at the dock by some of the staff. An ambulance crew was waiting with a stretcher.

Marshall's dad carried the sleeping boy off the plane and laid him on the stretcher. The crew strapped him down and pushed the stretcher across the dock to the waiting ambulance.

"Can Ethan ride with you?" Marshall's dad asked.

"Sure, no problem."

"Ethan, we'll take care of the stuff here and meet you at the hospital. We shouldn't be long."

"I'll be fine," Ethan said.

He climbed into the back of the ambulance and they drove out of the camp. The attendant checked Marshall's pulse and breathing. He listened to his lungs.

"He's full of fluid," he said shaking his head. "His temp is 102 so he's got a bad infection."

"Is it pneumonia?" Ethan asked.

"I think so but the docs will know for sure."

They arrived at the hospital and took Marshall to the emergency room. Ethan stopped at the desk to give them as much information as he could about Marshall. He explained that the dads were on the way so the nurse let him go to the emergency room.

They'd stripped Marshall's clothes off and he was lying on a bed with a sheet across his lower half. There was a large black and blue bruise on his right side. They'd inserted an IV into the back of his hand and had an oxygen tube strung under his nose feeding oxygen to him.

"Are you his brother?" the attending doctor asked.

"I'm his friend. I was with him when we crashed the plane. Our dads are on their way."

"He's a sick boy. His right lung is barely working. I'm going to do a chest X-ray to check his ribs and to see what's going on with that lung. I expect it's full of fluid.

Ethan nodded that he understood. "If you want to wait out in the reception area we'll come and get you when we're finished."

He walked out and sat on a worn couch. As he sat there he realized that he was starving. He walked up to the counter and inquired of the nurse where he could get something to eat and she pointed him to some machines down the hall. He got a can of soda and a candy bar and was walking back when the dads came into the waiting area.

"So how's he doing?" Marshall's dad asked.

"They're doing an X-ray right now. I talked to the doc and he said Marshall's right lung is bad. They'll let us know when they're done."

They all sat down and waited.

"Where did you get that?" his dad asked pointing to the soda.

"Down there, there are machines."

The dads walked down and both returned with a cup of coffee.

Just as they sat down the doctor came out of the emergency

room.

"Which of you is Marshall's dad?"

His dad stepped forward. "I'm his dad, how is he doing?"

"His worst problem is that he has pneumonia in his right lung. The left lung is fine. The pneumonia was probably caused when he ingested lake water when the plane crashed. Thankfully his left lung is fine so he's not in danger just yet. But we have to get that infection stopped. His ribs are bruised. I couldn't see any broken ribs. They're hard to see but I think he just got a good shot to the side as they crashed."

"So it's not from me doing chest compressions?" Ethan asked.

"No it's on the side, not where you'd have pushed too hard. Your compressions saved his life, and you didn't injure him," the doctor said smiling.

Ethan looked relieved.

"We're going to have to hospitalize him for a while. We'll need to treat him with strong antibiotics in his IV. He'll need oxygen for a while too. Do you have insurance that will cover it?"

"We have good insurance. Anything that isn't covered will be paid by us," Marshall's dad said.

"Okay, then if you will check with the nurse, we'll take him up to a room."

The dads went to the desk and Ethan followed the doctor.

"Is it okay that I come along?" he asked.

"Sure, he's all ready to go."

Ethan was shocked when he walked into the emergency room. Marshall was wearing a hospital gown and had an additional IV in his other arm. He had a tube running down his mouth that was taped to the side of his cheek. There was a bottle of fluid running into his IV and it was attached to a pole hooked to the bed. As the orderly helped the nurse get the bed through the doorway Ethan noticed a plastic bag hanging from the lower part of the bed. There was yellow fluid in it. His eyes got big when he realized what it was.

"Is that?" he said pointing.

The nurse nodded. "He has a catheter. We need him to be very quiet for a couple of days."

"Was he sleeping when you put that in his... in him?"

"Oh yes, he didn't feel a thing," she said smiling.

"Oh man," Ethan thought to himself. "Marshall is NOT going to like that."

He followed the orderly to a room where they parked Marshall's bed and the nurse connected a blood pressure cuff and a pulse monitor to him. She checked everything and then pulled the sheet up over his chest.

"Your friend is going to be fine. He's a strong young boy. Many people who come in here with pneumonia are old and already sick and it takes its toll, but he'll pull through just fine. He needs rest."

The nurse left and Ethan sat on a nearby chair and looked at his lifelong friend. "Dang he looks pretty pitiful," he said to himself. Then he thought about how close he had come to losing Marshall forever and his eyes filled with tears. "Thanks God, thanks for letting Marshall stay with us."

34

Ten minutes later the dads walked into the room. Marshall's dad walked up and held Marshall's hand and looked very sad. He looked over to Ethan.

"I haven't thanked you for saving him," he said. "If it hadn't been for you he'd be in that plane and he'd be dead."

"He would have done the same thing for me," Ethan said. "I was just lucky enough not to get knocked out. I'm really happy he's going to be alright."

"The doctor told us they want to keep him for 5 or 6 days."

"What are you going to do? You need to get back to the store."

"Well, we aren't sure yet."

"Listen, I can stay with Marshall. You two go back and we'll come when he's better."

"We talked about that. We were thinking that we could fly home and leave the car for you. We'll leave you plenty of money and when he's better you guys can drive back. Would that be okay with you?"

"Sure, I don't have anything I need to do at home for another month. Then I'll have to get ready to leave for boot camp. I'd rather stay here than be home worrying anyway."

"I called his mother and she thinks I should stay," Marshall's dad said. "But I told her that all anyone can do is stand by and wait. She thinks you'll do just fine."

"I'll be here and make sure he gets better," Ethan said.

Marshall's dad leaned over the bed and kissed his son on the forehead. He smiled at Ethan.

The dads left to go to the airport to see what they could find for tickets to Wisconsin. A nurse came in and checked Marshall. Ethan asked how he was doing and she said he seemed fine. His temp had gone up a little but that wasn't anything to worry about just yet. Ethan asked her if there was someplace close that was cheap where he could stay while Marshall was getting better.

"There's a little motel with cabins just down the street," she said. "They rent the cabins by the day or week. I'm sure they'd have something that wouldn't be too expensive. Just tell them what's going on and I know they'll be fair with you. I know them and they're real nice people."

Ethan thanked her for the information. A while later the dads came back told Ethan they had booked a flight to Milwaukee and then to Madison. Their wives would pick them up there.

"Here's money enough for you for the week and then some. I've given the desk nurse a form giving you power of attorney for Marshall just in case they need permission to do some procedure. Here's a credit card and the car keys. You'll have to buy some clothes too. We saw a big box store that looked like a place you could find some essentials. Is there anything else?"

Ethan told them about the little cabins down the street and they thought that was a good idea. Then Marshall's dad bent down and hugged his son as best he could and whispered into this ear. Ethan's dad hugged him.

"I'm very proud of you son. You stepped up and acted like the fine young man I knew you were."

His eyes were full when he kissed Ethan on the cheek.

"I'll take good care of him. I'll see if I can buy a Trac-Phone and I'll call you and let you know how it's going. My phone took a drink in the lake and is kaput."

"Use the credit card if you run out of cash. Just do whatever it takes to get both of you home safe," Marshall's dad said.

"I will, I promise."

After the dads had left Ethan decided he'd walk down the street to the motel and see about the room. There was a boy about Marshall's age in the office. Ethan explained about his situation and the kid listened.

"Let me go and get my mom," he said.

Soon he returned with an older lady. He'd told her Ethan's story and she was more than accommodating.

"We have a nice little one bed cabin that isn't being used. We'll put you in there and if no one comes to rent it you can have it for free. If we lose a rental we'll charge you for that day only."

"That's very generous of you," Ethan said.

"We're glad we can help," she said. "Luke take him and show him the cabin," she said to the boy.

Ethan followed the boy to the last cabin in the row. It was very small and quaint. They went inside.

"This is the kitchen, living room, dining room, bedroom and the toilet is behind that curtain."

Ethan grinned. "Just like home."

Luke laughed. "We didn't say it was luxurious. You can eat, sleep and crap and that's about all you need I think eh?"

Ethan laughed. "Yeah, that'll do."

"So do you have any luggage or anything?"

"All I have is the clothes I'm wearing," Ethan said. "Everything else I own is in the plane upside down at the lake."

"Which lake was it?"

"Marshall Lake. My friend who is hurt... his name is Marshall. What a coincidence huh?"

"Very strange eh?

Ethan grinned. He thought it was funny how Canadians always ended a sentence with eh."

"I think I should get back to the hospital. I want to be there if he wakes up."

Luke nodded. "When you come back stop at the office. If you want I'll show you around and maybe we can go and get a pizza or something. It'd be nice to have something to do for a change. This town is pretty boring if you know what I mean."

"That sounds great. Maybe you can show me a place to buy a few clothes so I won't stink up the place too."

"No problem eh."

35

E than entered Marshall's room just as a nurse was checking his vitals. He walked to the bed and looked at her with a questioning look on his face.

"His temp is down and that's good," she said. "Everything else looks like he's doing okay. Time will be the best healer."

"Is it okay if I just sit here with him?" Ethan asked.

"That's fine. Let us know if he wakes up."

Ethan sat in a chair near the bed and looked at Marshall lying there. He looked pretty rough. His brown hair was all snarled and sticking out. His face was very pale and his eyes looked sunken and looked almost like he had two black eyes.

"He looks kinda like a zombie," Ethan said to himself. "Poor kid, I wish I could do something for him."

Ethan laid his head back against the chair and within a couple of minutes he was asleep. He dreamed of the plane climbing up off the lake and how it twisted and turned in the strong gusts of wind. He saw the treetop coming and heard the screech of metal when the pontoon hit the trunk of the tree and spun the plane around. He woke with a start and looked toward the bed. Marshall was looking at him blinking his eyes.

"Hey, you're awake."

Marshall reached up with his hand and felt the tube that was taped to his cheek and going down his throat. He looked at Ethan with wide eyes.

"That's an oxygen tube. It's helping you breathe."

Marshall made a grunting noise and Ethan shook his head.

"I'll get the nurse, I don't know what you're saying."

He walked to the nurse's station and told the nurse that Marshall was awake. She followed him back to the room.

"So you're back with us. How are you feeling?"

Marshall touched the tube and shrugged.

"Let me get a white board for you," she said and left the

room.

Soon she came back and handed him the white board and a marker. Marshall wrote. "How long I need this tube?"

"I'll notify the doctor that you're awake. He'll come in and make that decision okay?"

Marshall nodded. The nurse walked out.

"The tube's pretty bad huh?" Ethan said.

"Horrible. Were is dad?"

"They left for home. They took a plane and left us the car. I'm staying at a little motel for now. When you're all better we'll drive home."

Marshall nodded. Just then the doctor came in and walked up to the bed.

"So, you're awake. That's good. He checked the chart and the readings on all of the machines. Then he gave the nurse some instructions and said he'd be back later to check on him.

"Okay we're going to turn down the flow on your oxygen tube. If you can breathe well enough without it we can remove it, but if not it has to stay, do you understand?"

Marshall nodded.

She punched some buttons on a machine and waited watching Marshall. He kept breathing like before. She punched the buttons some more and watched again. Soon she punched them again and Marshall's breathing didn't seem to change.

"I think you're okay," she said. "I've got it down to zero and you seem fine. How about I get that thing out of your throat?"

Marshall nodded vigorously.

She raised the head end of the bed up some and then took the tape off Marshall's cheek.

"Okay now, this will make you gag, so if you feel like you're going to throw up you can do it in this, she said putting a rectangular plastic container on his lap. "Are you ready?"

He looked a little scared but nodded.

She took hold of the tube and pulled. Ethan was amazed at

how long the tube was but finally the end of it popped out of his mouth. Marshall gagged a bit but managed not to throw up. His eyes watered and he was sweating but smiled at them.

Ethan picked up a towel that the nurse had brought in and wiped his face of sweat.

"Wow, that's better," he said with a hoarse voice.

"I knew you'd like that," the nurse said.

"No kidding."

Ethan was smiling. "Good to see you up," he said.

"Thanks, when is lunch?"

The nurse laughed. "Teenage boys. You can run over them, drop them from a building, crash a plane with them and they're still hungry. I'll see what I can scare up for you."

"How do your ribs feel?" Ethan asked.

"They're sore but I'll live. It's still hard to breathe."

Ethan nodded.

"How long have I been asleep?"

"A long time, you passed out when we took off from the lake."

Marshall shifted in the bed and suddenly he got a questioning look on his face. He put his hand under the covers and suddenly he got a surprised look.

"There's a tube in my wiener."

Ethan laughed. "That's a catheter. They did that while you were sleeping. It's so you don't have go get up and down to pee."

"But it's in my wiener," Marshall said again.

Ethan shrugged. "So?"

"Who put it there?"

"Probably a nurse."

"You mean a nurse was holding... are you sure?"

"Marshall, they see wieners every day, it's no big deal."

"Well, I'm not sure I like the idea of my wiener being paraded all over the place."

Ethan shook his head. It was going to be a long few days.

36

An aid came in a while later with a tray of food. She put it on the table that fit over the bed and Ethan pushed the button to raise the bed up so Marshall could eat. He took the covers off the tray. There was a piece of toast, a small dish of red Jello and a half a banana.

"Jeez they're going to starve me," Marshall said looking at the food.

"It's better than nothing. You better eat that and see how it settles. It might be enough after all."

Marshall began eating and by the time he'd eaten the toast and half of the Jello he was feeling a little queasy. He lay back on his pillow and closed his eyes.

"You better get that puke pail," he said.

Ethan grabbed the plastic tub and sat it on the edge of the bed. Marshall lay there a few minutes and then opened his eyes.

"I think I'm okay now. Whew, I thought I was gonna blow up."

"Hence the small amount of food the first time," Ethan said.

"Hence, wow you learned a new word."

Just then the doctor and a younger guy who looked like a doctor in training came in. The doctor introduced the younger guy as an intern.

"The X-ray shows about half a lung full of fluid in your right lung. The left one is clear so that's good. We're going to remove that fluid and then we can give you some drugs in an atomizer that will heal the inside of the lung."

"How are you going to get the fluid out?" Marshall asked.

"We'll use a large needle and go in through your back and suck it out."

Marshall's eyes got big. He looked at Ethan for help.

"I'm sure they numb you," Ethan said uncertainly.

"We numb the surface but it's hard to get the entire area numb. It's a pretty fast procedure so it'll be a little uncomfortable for a few minutes but you'll feel much better after we're done."

"Oh goodie," Marshall said.

A nurse came in pushing a cart with many instruments on it. They had Marshall sit up on the edge of the bed with his feet on the floor. Then they took his gown down off his top half of his body and the nurse began cleaning his back. She washed him all down and then swabbed the area with iodine. The doctor told the intern to find a certain rib and the young guy felt with his gloved hands until he found the spot. He marked it with a pen. Then the doctor felt the same area and nodded.

"You found the right place," he said.

"Okay Marshall you'll feel a little pinch now as we numb the area," he said.

Ethan stepped up to Marshall and held onto his hands as they stuck a needle with anesthesia several times into his back. He jumped when they stuck him but didn't say anything. They waited a few minutes and then the doctor poked him in the back with a needle.

"Did you feel that?"

"What?"

"You're ready," he said.

Then he instructed the young guy on how to insert the needle and remove the fluid.

Marshall turned his head and saw the needle and plastic cylinder that was attached to it.

"Holy crap, that's like a horse needle," he said.

"Sorry, we'll be as gentle as we can," the young guy said.

"Have you done this before?" Marshall asked.

"Um, no, this is my first time. But I practiced on cadavers and I got an A- on my technique."

Marshall looked at Ethan and mouthed the word cadavers.

Ethan burst out laughing. "Sorry," he said.

"Maybe I should wait out in the hall," Ethan said.

"It's up to you," the intern said to Marshall.

"Are you afraid you'll faint?" Marshall asked grinning.

"I hope not. If I feel light in the head I'll sit down so I don't fall and crack my head open."

"Okay, let'er rip doc."

Marshall gasped as the needle went into his back. He reached out to Ethan and put his head against Ethan's chest. Ethan held him tightly. The intern pushed the needle through the tissue between two ribs and into the space surrounding his lung and then into the lower part of the lung. Once it was in he withdrew the plunger and sucked a yellowish fluid out until the cylinder was full. The doctor replaced the full cylinder with an empty one and they sucked out another tube full of fluid. They replaced that cylinder and got half of another one.

Then the intern removed the needle and they wiped the hole off and put a bandage over the spot.

Marshall was sweating and looked a little shaken but held up pretty well. "Done?" he asked.

"Yes, we're done and you did a fine job."

They helped him lay back down in the bed. Already he could feel his breath coming easier.

"The nurse will bring in an inhaler for you with some medicine in it. You take it as she instructs and I'll be back before bedtime to see how you're doing. They'll come down later and get another chest X-ray and we'll see how things are," the doctor said.

Marshall thanked him and told the intern he did a good job and they left.

"I'm glad that's over with," he said.

"I hurt and I was just watching," Ethan said grinning.

"Well, if it'll get me out of here sooner I'm glad they did it."

He lay there a minute and then yawned. "I think I'll take a

nap," he said sleepily.

"Okay, I'll leave you alone. I'm going to go and get us some clothes for when you're all healed up so we have something to wear on the way home."

"Cool, get me some cargo shorts and some new flip flops. If I have two or three tee shirts and some boxers I'll be in good shape."

"No problem. I'll see you later. Get some rest." He started for the door and Marshall's eyes were closed before he left the room.

37

E than stopped the car in front of the office at the motel. He went inside and Luke was watching a small television in the back of the room. When he saw Ethan walk in he turned off the TV and called to his mom that he was taking Ethan to get some clothes and stuff.

"So do you have a Walmart or something like that?" Ethan asked.

"Not a Walmart eh, but something like it."

They got in the car and Luke directed Ethan to the store. It was much like a Walmart or Kmart but a bit smaller. They went inside and Ethan picked out some tee shirts in size medium for Marshall and a pair of tan cargo shorts and one pair of white ones with big blue flowers on them. He also got him a six-pack of boxers in size medium and a pair of size 10 flip-flops. He got the same stuff for himself in size large except for the flowered shorts. He substituted a pair made of camouflage material.

Then he got each of them a toothbrush, he also bought a tube of toothpaste and a can of Axe "Stink-Me-Pretty", as Marshall called deodorant. They wandered through the store and he picked up a bag of Snicker bars and some Gator Aid drinks.

"Well I think that'll do it," he said.

"Are you hungry?" Luke asked.

"I'm starved. What do you have in mind?"

"There's a good pizza joint down the road here, or we could go to a burger place, whichever you feel like eating," Luke said.

"I'm starving for pizza. We were at the lake for a week and we ate fish every day. I like fish but I'm ready for something a little more spicy right now."

They checked out and drove to the pizza store. Inside Luke ran into some of his friends and they invited them to sit with them. They had just arrived and hadn't ordered yet.

"This is Ethan. He's staying at our place. He was on a fishing trip and their pilot crashed the plane. His friend is in the hospital with pneumonia," Luke explained.

The other kids, three boys and four girls all had many questions and were very friendly. One of the girls, a blond with beautiful blue eyes was especially friendly and it was obvious she was flirting.

"Watch out," Luke whispered. "She's a Black Widow spider."

Ethan laughed. "You think I'm in danger?"

"Only if you want to be," Luke said grinning.

They ordered several pizzas and spent the next hour eating and talking. Ethan felt right at home and it was nice to just sit and be a kid for a while instead of having to be responsible all the time. After a while though he felt he should go and see how Marshall was doing so he excused himself and said he needed to go to the hospital and check on his friend. Luke rode with him.

"That blond, Dianna, she's a hot one," Ethan said.

"That she is," Luke said. "She's got more notches on her belt than most sailors."

"Really? She seems very sweet and innocent."

Luke laughed. "Every guy at that table has been involved with her at one time or another."

Ethan looked over at Luke. "You too?"

Luke grinned. "Me too."

When they got to the hospital Ethan carried Marshall's clothes up to his room in the store bag. He stuffed a bunch of the Snickers and sodas into the bag too. Marshall was lying and watching TV when they walked in.

"Hey Marsh, how's it going?" Ethan asked.

"Good, I'm feeling a lot better now that they got that stuff out of my lung. Who's this?" he said looking at Luke.

Ethan introduced them and they got along immediately. Marshall looked through his goodies and was impressed with the blue and white shorts.

"I didn't think you had such good taste," he said holding them up.

"I've known you for 16 years, I think I know your taste," Ethan said.

Just then the doctor came in and checked all of Marshall's vital signs. He listened to his lungs and nodded.

"You're sounding pretty good," he said. "I think we'll get that catheter out so you can start taking short walks in the hallway. We want you to go all the way to the end and back without stopping and then you should be good to go."

Marshall was glad to hear that. The doctor left and he turned to Ethan.

"Do they put you to sleep to take that hose out of my special thing?"

Ethan burst out laughing. "What so special about it?"

"Well I'm pretty fond of it, so it's special to me."

"I don't know Marshall but I doubt they'd put you to sleep to take it out."

They didn't have to wait long to find out. A nurse came into the room and walked up to the bed. She was in her mid-twenties and very pretty.

"So I guess you're ready to be free of that urine bag," she said.

Marshall nodded and looked at Ethan with a look of terror.

"Do you two want to step out for a second?" she asked.

Ethan and Luke were only too happy to leave. As they got to the door Ethan stopped and gave Marshall a thumbs-up.

"We'll let's get that out of you," the nurse said. She pulled back the covers and pulled his gown up. Then she put a syringe into a little tube on the side of the tube that was running into his bladder. "I'm letting the air out of a little bulb on the end so it'll pull out easily," she said.

Marshall nodded but he was trying to think of being

someplace else.

Then she took hold of his "special thing" and pulled and the tube slid out. Marshall cringed a bit. It didn't really hurt but it felt pretty strange. Then it was over and she was covering him back up.

"All done," she said.

Marshall could tell that his face was red. He felt really flushed.

"Okay, thank you," he said blushing.

"Don't worry sweetie, I've done that hundreds of times and I've never seen a guy yet who felt differently than you do. You did just fine. And for the record, you're equipped just fine."

She walked from the room and Ethan and Luke came in looking expectantly.

"So how did it go?" Ethan asked.

"She just grabbed it and pulled the tube out," Marshall said.

"She grabbed it?"

"Yeah, and she said I've got nothing to worry about equipment-wise."

"She said that?"

"Yeah, she said that."

"She was probably just being nice," Luke said.

Marshall looked at the new kid. "Jeez you're as bad as Ethan."

They all began laughing.

38

The days passed and Marshall's health improved. His color was back to normal and his chest X-rays showed no new fluid in his lung. The doctor told him to walk the halls several times a day and that was what he was doing when Ethan and Luke came to see him.

"Hey you're looking good," Ethan said when he saw Marshall walking along toward them pushing a little roller stand that had his IV bag hanging from it. He was grinning and wearing his new flip-flops.

"Yeah, I'm doing about ten laps of the hallway at a time now. I'm not even tired when I get done."

"You'll be ready to go home soon then," Luke said.

"The doc says maybe tomorrow," Marshall said.

"We brought you some pizza," Ethan said lifting the bag he was carrying.

"Oh boy, I'm starving too," Marshall said hurrying toward them.

They stepped aside and he passed them and headed to his room. Ethan and Luke began laughing as Marshall led them to the room.

"You know that your rear end is hanging out," Ethan said chuckling.

Marshall looked over his shoulder. "I thought I'd give the girls a little thrill."

While he was eating his pizza Marshall's doctor came in and checked him over.

"I think we can let you go home tomorrow," he said. "Everything looks good. I'll write a couple of prescriptions for you and you're good to go."

Marshall thanked him for all he'd done and they made plans for Ethan to pick him up first thing the next morning.

Ethan and Luke went back to the motel and hung out in Ethan's little cabin.

"I'm glad Marshall's better but I hate to see you go," Luke said. "It's been nice having someone to hang with."

"I'm glad I got to meet you," Ethan said. "It would have been a long week all by myself. If you ever get the chance to come to Wisconsin, let me know and we'll show you around."

They exchanged each other's emails and phone numbers and Luke said goodnight. He had to open in the morning so Ethan said he'd stop by and say goodbye then.

The next morning Ethan checked out and bid Luke and his mom goodbye. He thanked them for all they'd done for him. What he didn't tell them was that he'd left $100 in an envelope in the cabin.

Marshall was dressed and ready to go. They said goodbye to all of the nurses and other people at the hospital that they'd gotten to know during the week. Many of the nurses had to hug and kiss him goodbye.

They settled in the car and Ethan headed down the highway toward home. Marshall was a little quiet.

"What's wrong?" Ethan asked.

"Oh nothing. I'm glad to be going home, but I'm sad that Derrick died. I'm happy to be seeing our parents but I'm sad that you'll be leaving soon. It's kind of a happy/sad thing."

"Well, you know we have to move on Marsh," Ethan said. "Life goes on."

"Yeah, I know, but that doesn't make it any easier."

They crossed the border and stopped at a McDonalds. They were both pretty hungry for a quarter-pounder.

"Mmm," Marshall said, "Now I know we're home."

They pulled into the driveway just after dark. The parents were all there waiting because Ethan had called ahead and let them know they were on the way. Buzzie just about turned inside out when he saw Marshall. He whined and licked his beloved master as Marshall tried to get into the house. They spent the next few hours catching up on Marshall's adventures in the hospital and Buzzie never left his side. He left out the part about the catheter.

Everyone was getting tired so they all went to their home and off to bed. Marshall was playing ball with Buzzie and he was sitting on his bed when he noticed Ethan come into his room across the way. Ethan slipped off his shoes and shirt and then went into the bathroom. Marshall figured he was taking a shower because he was in there quite a while. Finally he came out, his hair wet and wearing a pair of boxers. He sprawled on his bed and picked up his remote and turned the TV on. He searched through the channels and found a hockey game and lay back to watch it.

"I really shouldn't," Marshall thought.

He picked up his remote and pointed it at Ethan's TV. He pushed the numbers for CNN. Ethan's TV switched.

"What the?" Ethan grabbed his remote and switched it back.

Marshall waited a bit and when one team was charging toward a goal he switched it to FOX.

"You freaking thing!"

Ethan grabbed his remote and jammed his finger on it changing the channel back. Then he stopped and looked down it the remote. He turned and looked across the yard and caught Marshall standing there with his remote in his hand.

"You little shit. You've been doing this for months and I didn't figure it out till now."

Marshall was laughing so hard he could barely stand up. Ethan pulled his shades down and shut off the light. Marshall patted the bed and Buzzie jumped up and curled up next to him. "We got him again Buzzie," he said.

He'd barely shut his eyes and he was deeply sleeping.

Ethan watched until he saw Marshall's light go out. Then he pulled on his shorts and snuck across the yard. He tiptoed into the kitchen and up to Marshall's room. Buzzie sat up when Ethan slipped into the room but Ethan whispered to him to lie back down and the dog obeyed.

There was enough light for him to see Marshall lying on his back, mouth slightly open snoring away. He reached into his pocket and removed a little shaver/trimmer. He turned it on and it made a buzzing sound but it wasn't very loud.

"I shouldn't do this," he chuckled. "But I'm gonna anyway."

He leaned over the bed and shaved off Marshall's left eyebrow. Buzzie watched, fascinated as Ethan did his work.

He patted the dog on the head. "Good boy," he whispered. He went to the window and opened the shade so he'd be able to see into Marshall's bedroom in the morning.

Then he snuck back downstairs, out of the house and back to his bedroom. He opened his shade and set his alarm for 7am.

"There's no way he'll wake up before then," he thought. He was grinning from ear to ear as he lay down and went to sleep.

39

Marshall woke when he smelled something terrible. He opened his eyes and Buzzie was lying next to him with his butt right next to Marshall's face. The little dog had dropped a fart bomb.

"Jeez Buzzie, that stinks," he whined.

The dog looked up, sniffed the air and snorted and then lay back down and closed his eyes. Marshall just shook his head.

"He has to be the fartingest dog in the world," he thought to himself. He rolled over and noticed a lot of short dark hairs on his pillow.

"Buzzie are you shedding?" he asked. The dog snorted and slept on. Marshall brushed the hairs off his pillow. "I'll have to give you a bath today," he said.

He got up and looked across the yard and saw Ethan reading a book in his room. He yawned and shuffled off to the bathroom to take a shower. He didn't even bother to turn on the light, but dropped his boxers and turned on the water. Once it got to the temperature he liked, he got in and showered and washed his hair. He shut the water off and grabbed a towel and dried off. The mirror was covered with steam so he wiped a spot off with his towel. He put on some deodorant and ran his fingers through his hair giving that "slept in" look. Just as he turned to leave he stopped and looked into the mirror again. His mouth dropped open and he reached up to the left side of his forehead and touched the stubble of where his eyebrow had been.

"What the? Ethan!" It had to be him. At first he started for the door to declare war but then he stopped. "Maybe I need to just ignore it. He'll go nuts and be scared to death of retaliation," he thought. He decided that was what he'd do.

He walked into the room wrapped in his towel and got a pair of boxers from his dresser. Then he made a big show of turning his butt toward Ethan and bending over to put them on. When he stood back up he caught Ethan quickly looking back into his book.

"Hey, what're you reading?"

"Oh uh, it's a book about military dogs. It's what gave me the idea of being a dog handler. How are you feeling today?"

"I'm good, just like new."

"Good so everything's okay?"

"Everything's great except for one thing," he said.

"What's that?" Ethan said grinning.

"I'm starved. Have you eaten breakfast yet?"

Ethan looked a little flustered. "Um no, I haven't."

"I'll make us some scrambled eggs and bacon, okay?"

"Sure, you sure everything is okay?

"Of course, I'm great. Come over in about 15 minutes," he said.

Ethan nodded.

Marshall grinned and said to himself, "Yeah, come on over and I'll feed you some breakfast."

He went downstairs and started on the breakfast. First he fried some bacon and then poured off part of the fat. Then he cracked three eggs into a bowl and whipped them up. Then he did the same to three more eggs in a second bowl. He opened the refrigerator and found what he was looking for. He took out one green pepper and one jalapeno pepper. He chopped both of them up keeping them separate. Then he chopped some onion.

He got a carton of milk out of the fridge and poured some of it into the blender. Then he poured in some chocolate syrup. He blended the two and poured half of the mixture into one glass and then added a big spoon of cayenne pepper to the other half, blended it and poured it into the other glass.

He scrambled one bowl of eggs with the green pepper and put them on a plate and then did the others with the jalapeno. He was just putting them on the plate when Ethan walked in through the back door. He was still barefoot and was wearing shorts and a tank top.

"Are you ready Iron Chef?"

"You timed it just right," Marshall said.

Ethan sat at the table and looked at the spread. "Very nice, even chocolate milk," he said.

"I'm just glad to be home and have time to spend with you until you go. We won't have too many more mornings together you know."

Ethan had a hard time not laughing at Marshall's bare forehead. He had to have noticed it. "So everything's good today? You feeling okay and everything?"

"Yeah, good except one thing, Buzzie farted in my bed and nearly killed me in my sleep. He's shedding. There were short hairs all over my pillow."

Ethan almost burst out laughing but shoved a big forkful of eggs into his mouth to cover his laughter. He chewed and suddenly something seemed to be wrong. His mouth was on fire. He swallowed the eggs and looked confused.

"Are the eggs okay?" Marshall asked.

"Yeah, they're great," Ethan said taking another forkful of them. Now his throat was on fire too. He broke out in a sweat and swallowed the second bite of eggs. "These are pretty spicy," he said.

"Really? I didn't notice. Have some chocolate milk, that'll cool you off."

Ethan picked up his glass and gulped in about half of the milk. He swallowed it and started choking. "Holy shit, what's in that?" he gasped.

"It's just milk and chocolate syrup and a touch of cayenne for some zip."

"A touch! My mouth is on fire. What's in the eggs??

"Just eggs and a bit of jalapeno. And maybe an eyebrow hair or two."

Ethan was sweating and his face was all red. He went to the refrigerator and grabbed the jug of milk and drank half of it. He let a big burp and looked at Marshall.

"You turd, you tried to kill me."

"Only after you defaced me. Look at my face. What am I suppose to do for the time it takes to grow eyebrow back?"

Now Ethan was grinning. "I'll buy you a magic marker and you can paint one on."

That struck Marshall as funny and he burst out laughing. He stood up and put out his hand. "How about a truce until you leave for the Marines?" Ethan took his hand and then pulled him to his chest and hugged him.

"Okay truce," he said. Then he hugged his friend harder. "I'm really going to miss you Marsh," he whispered.

Marshall nodded but said nothing, knowing that if he spoke he'd start to cry. They stood there hugging for a several minutes, not saying anything. Nothing needed to be said.

40

The weeks passed quickly and soon they were looking at Ethan's departure day. The evening before he was to leave, the two families had gone out to a fancy restaurant and had an expensive dinner, but avoided talking about Ethan leaving. When they got home the parents went out on the patio for a drink and the two boys were left alone.

"So, what time are we leaving for the airport?" Marshall asked.

"My flight leaves at 10:30 so I'm suppose to be there at least an hour early, so I think we're going to leave at about 8am."

"So do you have everything you need?" Marshall asked.

"I don't need much," Ethan said. "Once I get there I'll get clothes and boots and everything else, so all I'm really taking is my phone and some money and my laptop. I'm hoping they'll have a place for us to get the Internet so I can talk to you and the folks on Skype."

Marshall nodded. "That'll be good," he said.

They sat silently for a minute. "Hey did you think about trying out for the play?"

Marshall nodded. "I'm going to do it. The try-outs are next week. I might get one of the "peasant" parts."

"You'll do great. You've got a good voice."

"Yeah, but it'd be more fun if you were here to see it."

Ethan smiled sadly. "It'll be okay Marsh. You're going to be a senior next year so you'll have lots to do. If you get a part in the play you'll really be busy. You've got other friends so there'll be lots for you to keep you involved, and you'll probably forget all about me."

"Don't even say that," Marshall said. "Don't ever even think that."

They hugged and then Marshall walked home and went to his room. Buzzie was happy to see him and jumped up on the bed and tried to get him to play. Marshall picked up the little dog and buried his face in his coat and cried. Buzzie licked his face and cuddled up to him as if he knew something was wrong.

The next morning they left for the airport right on time. Ethan's parents were in the front seat and the two boys were in the back. Marshall's parents had said their goodbyes at the house.

"You've got your credit card?" his dad asked.

"Yeah, I'm good Dad, I won't have to spend much money for a while, they give you everything from underwear to shoes."

"Well if you do need anything, you've got the card."

Ethan grinned at Marshall.

When they got to the airport Ethan checked in and got his boarding pass and found which gate he needed to go to.

They got to the security checkpoint and Ethan's mom and dad hugged him and said goodbye. They stepped back and Marshall stood there feeling very empty inside. Ethan put his big strong arms around him and hugged him hard. "I'll see you in about 8 months," he said.

Marshall nodded. "I miss you already," he whispered.

"Be strong, I'll be back before you know it."

Marshall nodded and Ethan broke the embrace and turned and went through the security check. He picked up his duffle bag on the other side and walked away. When he got to the doorway that led to this gate he turned and waved, and then he walked out of sight.

Marshall felt like his heart was going to break. Ethan's mom put her arm around his shoulder and smiled at him.

"He'll be back in no time," she said.

"Yeah, I guess so," he said.

They walked out of the airport and drove home.

Ethan found his seat and stowed his bag in the over-head storage. There was a middle-aged man sitting next to him and a young boy next to him by the window. They began to chat and Ethan said he was on his way to boot camp. The man was an ex-marine and was very happy that Ethan was doing what he was doing.

"You'll never forget your service," he said. "Even boot camp."

"Is it bad?"

"You look like you're in good shape, you'll do fine. Just don't let your drill instructor get to you. They try to get into your head and drive you crazy. They're making you tough, though."

The heat was oppressive when Ethan got off the plane and walked out of the airport. He'd never been in South Carolina before and it was much hotter than it was in Wisconsin. He walked to a bus that was waiting outside the terminal. A Marine in camouflage fatigues was gathering several recruits who were arriving in the next couple of hours.

Ethan walked up to the middle-aged man and gave him his name. The man checked him off and told him where to put his duffle. "Welcome to Parris Island recruit," the soldier said.

"Thank you sir," Ethan replied.

"I'm not a Sir. I'm an enlisted man. I work for a living. You can call me Gunnery Sergeant Holt. I will be your momma, your daddy and your best friend for the next 12 weeks. And if you screw up I will be your worst enemy, do you understand?"

"Yes Gunnery Sergeant," Ethan said.

"Mazel tov, now get on the bus."

There were half a dozen other recruits on the bus already. Ethan found an empty seat and slid into it. The kid across the aisle smiled at him and slid over closer.

"Trant Skenner," he said extending his hand.

"Ethan Randall," Ethan said shaking hands with the kid. "So where are you from Trant?" he asked.

"It's T R E N T," the kid said, "I'm from southern Illinois," he drawled. It sounded like "sthn ill in oah".

"I'm from Wisconsin," Ethan said.

"Cool, we'ze neighbors," his new friend said.

Soon some of the others introduced themselves and in no time the bus filled with guys from all over the eastern half of the country. Recruits from east of the Mississippi took their basic training in South Carolina and the recruits from the west of the Mississippi went to San Diego.

"Ok, ladies," Gunnery Sergeant Holt said loudly from the front of the bus. "All of you seem to be here, at least in body, so we will now take the sunset tour of Parris Island training facility. Kindly keep your stupid heads and hands inside the bus or some real Marine may shoot them off. Understood?"

"Yes Gunnery Sergeant."

"Well done."

And the bus pulled out headed for the base. Ethan was excited but also a little apprehensive. "I wonder what Marshall is doing?" he thought as they drove down the road.

41

T he next few hours were a haze for Ethan and the new recruits. They were taken to their new barracks and were told to stow their gear and report to the front of the building in 5 minutes.

Trent asked Ethan if he minded if he took one of the bunks and Ethan was glad to let him chose. He took the top bunk. They stowed their duffle bags in lockers next to the beds and walked outside. All of the recruits were milling around when Gunnery Sergeant Holt walked out and bellowed at them to line up on the edge of the paved street that ran in front of their barracks. There was a lot of confusion and finally they all got lined up.

"We will now go to the induction center where you ladies will be sworn in, given uniforms and get a haircut. There will be no talking, no laughing, no nothing. Understood?"

"Yes Gunnery Sergeant Holt," they said.

"You may call me Gunny Holt, or Sergeant Holt, either is fine. Now move out."

They walked in single file across the base to the induction center. An officer read their oath and they all repeated it. They were now Marines.

Then they went into a big building and a crew of other Marines who worked there took their clothes sizes, shoe sizes and asked them if they wanted boxers or briefs. Ethan chose boxers. Behind him Trent also opted for boxers.

"I like my boys to have some room," he whispered to Ethan. Ethan grinned but said nothing.

They then went to a room where their blood pressure, and other vitals were measured. Then they went to another room where there were dentists who examined each of them. Finally they made a line in the next room and were told to drop their pants. A doctor went from recruit to recruit and asked them to cough as he checked them for hernias. Then they had to bend and he checked the other end.

Ethan looked to the left and Trent was grinning. "How'd ya lak to have this job?"

"Shh, you're gonna get us in trouble."

"Do you girls have something to share?"

The voice came from behind him. It was Gunny Holt.

"No Gunny Holt, I was just clearing my throat," Ethan said.

"Well clear it silently next time Randall or you'll be giving me a hundred pushups."

"Yes Gunny Holt."

Trent grinned and mouthed, "Sorry."

When they left the medical area they were each given a bundle of clothing, a pair of boots, a pair of sneakers and a bag with a toothbrush and other essentials. They lined up outside the barbershop and took turns going in and getting their heads shaved. Ethan didn't mind. He knew it was coming and even though he'd always had fairly long curly hair it was no big deal to him. His hair had always been naturally curly and it was easy to take care of when it was longer so that's why he let it grow. His mom would probably be more distressed than he was.

Once they were all done with haircuts they walked in line back to the barracks and were told to stow their gear, and dress in shorts and a tee shirt ready for a run. They had 5 minutes to be in line.

This time Gunny Holt had them line up in rows and did a lot of yelling when they didn't know for sure where to stand and how. It didn't take long and they were all lined up and Gunny Holt led them down the street on a slow jog.

Ethan had no problem keeping up but some of the guys were in less shape and soon began to pant and sweat. Holt yelled at them and kept them running. They got to the drill field and he had them stop and rest. Then they had to do 50 pushups. Ethan didn't have any trouble but many of the guys had a hard time after about 20 repetitions. Once the pushups were done they did sit-ups and then jumping jacks. And then they ran back to the barracks.

"Ok ladies. Hit the showers. Be lined up here at 1730 hours and we'll jog to the mess hall."

They went into the barracks and Ethan was tired but not nearly as tired as many of the others were. Trent was in good spirits.

"Yall r in good shape," he said.

"I did a lot of sports so I kept in shape," Ethan said.

"Ah worked for my Daddy loggin cumpnee, so Ahm in pretty good shape too."

"Some of the guys are hurting," Ethan said looking at one guy who was a bit overweight. He looked like he was ready to cry.

"That chubby gah, he's prolly thinking he made a big mistake rat now."

Ethan nodded.

They went to the showers and cleaned up and then dressed in their fatigues and got ready for chow. Ethan was hungry and hoped the chow was better than the haircut.

During the next few weeks they marched and ran and did push ups and climbed ropes and then did it all again hundreds of times. The chubby guy was now lean and mean and the others were all the same. Ethan had a good build when he got there but his shoulders and arms were now strongly muscled and he was lean and as strong as he'd ever been.

They learned hand-to-hand combat, they learned to shoot, and they learned to kill with a knife, or a club or with their hands. There were hours of classes in logistics and ballistics and language.

All recruits were required to take a class in learning basic terms and greetings in Arabic since they most likely would all end up in a middle-east country eventually. While some had a hard time Ethan found that he excelled in Arabic. Most of the troops were taught a few basic words but Ethan was such a quick learner that his instructor sent him to an advanced class. There he learned advanced phrases and words and a good lot about the culture of the Middle East.

The other guys in his squad became like brothers to him and he to them. They were together 24/7 and learned that the squad was only as strong as it's weakest member. Near the end of the 12 weeks of basic training Ethan was called to the office of the base commander.

He reported to the office and was directed to wait for someone to come and take him back. Soon a corporal came and got him and took him to the office of a captain.

He stepped in and announced himself and stood at attention.

"At ease Randall," the officer said. "Have a seat."

Ethan sat and waited to see what this was about.

"So they tell me you're very good at what you do."

"I'm not sure who they is but I'm glad they think I'm doing a good job Sir."

"You've mastered a good amount of Arabic?"

"Yes sir, it seems to come easy to me. I took 4 years of Spanish in high school and think that helped. I'm far from fluent in Arabic but I know quite a few phrases and words. I think I know enough to communicate on a low level."

"That's good. I see here that when you talked to your recruiter you showed interest in being a military dog handler."

"Yes sir, I'd like that very much," Ethan said.

"You know that most dog handlers are 3rd or 4th year people. We very seldom give a dog to a new recruit."

Ethan's spirits sank. "Oh they didn't tell me that at the recruiter's office Sir."

"I suppose not," the officer said smiling. "But you pose an unusual situation. You speak a good amount of Arabic and we have a special dog that needs a handler who can increase trust and friendship among the local people."

"I'm not sure I understand Sir."

"Most of our dogs are German Shepherds, and Belgian Malinois. These are kind of fierce looking dogs and are often used for crowd control as well as sniffing and attacks. The Muslim people are not dog people. They feel that dogs are unclean and are mostly afraid of them. They're especially afraid of the Shepherds and Malinios. They're pretty intense dogs. Then you add a big tough-looking Marine and they are pretty imposing. But occasionally we come across a dog with an amazing nose who will make a great sniffing dog but isn't what you'd expect to see. We get some Labradors and a few hounds, and while they make great sniffing dogs they aren't very scary. This particular dog that I'm talking about is a dog that has as good of a nose as any that have been in the program. It's also a very intelligent dog. But it's a dog that doesn't scare anyone."

"What is it? A poodle or something?"

"Oh hell no, not a poodle. It's a golden retriever. You know what these dogs look like. They're beautiful have a smile on their faces and a disposition like a kitten. But this guy has a nose that is remarkable. He needs a handler that can use him not only to sniff out explosives but a handler that can make friends with the locals and maybe get some good intelligence on the side. We are looking to partner him with a less-imposing soldier who might be able to make friends within the local community where he might be able to gather intelligence. He needs a non-threatening soldier who speaks the same language as the locals."

"I'm not threatening?"

"I'm sure you're as well trained and ready for battle as anyone here. Some of these guys look mean and scare the populace. Don't take the wrong, but you look kind of boyish Randall. There's nothing wrong with that. You'd make a good partner with this dog and we think it might produce intelligence that could save lives. Some of the younger local people would be easy for a guy like you to become friendly with, and that might produce some intelligence that could save lives."

"So you're saying that even though I'm not a 3rd year or 4th year, I could get a dog since I know Arabic?"

"I'm saying that and that a kid that has your looks and disposition would make an amazing partner with this dog. You're young and look very friendly. I've talked to Gunny Holt. He's been keeping an eye on you and he says you're a damn good soldier. No griping, no excuses, no lagging. He says he wishes he had a whole squad like you. And if you repeat that I'll see to it that you clean toilets for a month."

Ethan grinned. "Gunny Holt said something nice about me? Wow. Well Sir, I wanted to be a dog handler and if you think this dog and I will make a good pair, I'm in."

"Good deal." The Captain stood and they shook hands. "I'll see to the paperwork Randall."

Ethan walked from the office and felt like his feet weren't even touching the ground on the way back to the barracks. When he walked in Gunny Holt was in his office and he looked up as Ethan stopped at the door.

"So?"

"Thanks Gunny," Ethan said.

42

"**S**o they's gonna give yall a dog Aythan?" Trent asked as they were putting away their gear after a drill.

"It sounds like I'm in," Ethan said.

"Dang, that'd be nace. I got ma a old hound at home, name's Critter, he's not real perty but he sure can track coons."

Ethan grinned. "This dog is a golden retriever."

"Oh they's perty. I got a buddy what's got one, name is Beverley."

Ethan laughed. "Its name is Beverley? Jeez that's unusual."

"His granny's name is Beverley too. I think he named it after his granny."

"Well I hope my dog's name is something normal like Duke or Spike," Ethan said.

They were only a few days away from boot camp graduation. After that some of the guys would report to other bases for special training and some would remain in Parris Island. Ethan would be reporting to Lackland AF Base, which was where the dog program was conducted. He had made friends with a lot of the guys and knew he'd miss seeing some of them.

After the ceremony his squad members went back to the barracks and gathered their gear for their new assignments. Trent was going to infantry so he'd remain at Parris Island. Ethan was ready to get on a bus that would take him to the airport and he shook hands with Trent and said his farewell.

"Yall watch for me in Afghanistan," Trent said.

"I will, you keep your head down," Ethan said.

"Never fear that."

On the way out Gunny Holt was sitting in his office reading a report so Ethan stopped to say goodbye.

"Ready to go Randall?"

"Yes Gunny. I just wanted to thank you for all the fun."

Gunny Holt looked up and grinned. "Its kind of fun if you're smart and in good shape like you are Randall. Not so much fun for those dopes that show up here soft and fat. But they're good now."

"I wanted to thank you for the good words getting me into the dog program."

"You'll make a great team with a dog. You can do a lot of good. Just be careful, trust your dog but keep alert. Those bad guys over there come up with something new all the time. Just when you think you've got them figured out, they do something different. Keep your head down Marine. HooRa!"

"HooRa, Gunny."

Ethan had a lump in his throat as he walked to his seat on the bus. He was going to miss the Sergeant even though the last 12 weeks had been some of the hardest of his life.

He arrived at Lackland six hours later. There was a bus at the airport picking up recruits so he got on board.

At the base he reported to the main office and was directed to the Military Dog Training Facility.

He walked into the barracks and found several other guys putting away their gear. One of them walked up to him.

"You a dog guy?" he asked.

"Yeah, Ethan Randall," he said extending his hand.

"You're the young guy for Russell," the older man said.

"Russell?"

"Russell is your dog. He's easy to pick out from the others. He's not nasty and snarling. He actually smiles."

"I was told he had a good nose."

"I don't know about that. These dogs all have good noses. Some are just more intimidating than others. Shepherds are big, fierce looking and have huge teeth. Malinois are smaller but have a black face that looks angry and hold on with a bite like an alligator. In fact we call them Mali-gators."

Ethan laughed. "I've never seen one I don't think," he said.

"Oh you'll be impressed. They're small but very very intimidating.

The other guy showed him where to stow his gear and soon more dog handlers arrived. They were all chatting and getting to know each other when a Sergeant walked in. "Attention!"

They all snapped to attention.

"I am Master Sergeant Romero. Most of you guys are seasoned veterans of one or more tours of duty. You know the drill. I am not here to baby sit you. I will watch and evaluate you and if you do not hold up to the level we expect, you will not be a dog handler.

"Your dog is not your pet. Your dog is a soldier just like you are. Your dog will outrank you. If you are ever caught striking a superior officer, you will be court marshaled. Your dog will do as you tell it, so make damn sure you know what you are doing and do not ask your dog to do something that will cause it harm. Are there any questions?"

No one said a word.

"Ok then fall out and form a squad and we'll quick march over to the kennels and you can meet your new partners."

Ethan and the others formed up and they jogged across the base to the dog training area. The entire area was fenced with cyclone fencing and inside there was a large low building with kennel runs outside all the way around. In the runs there were dogs all watching them. Some of the dogs lay on the cement and others stood and barked. Almost all of them were German Shepherds and Belgian Malinois. Ethan looked for a Golden Retriever but didn't see one.

Sergeant Romero led them into the building where another Sergeant met them.

"I am Master Sergeant Shepherd."

A few of the men laughed.

"Go ahead, I've heard it all before. A Sergeant named Shepherd in charge of dogs. Great joke. You can call me Sarge

Shepherd. I'm good with that."

They all nodded.

"But... If I ever see one of you mistreat one of my dogs... If I ever see you hit one of my dogs... If I ever see you do anything to one of my dogs... You will see the angriest man you've ever had the occasion to meet. You will respect these dogs. You will treat these dogs as well or better as you would your own brother. You will see to their needs before you see to your needs. Are there any questions?"

"No Sarge Shepherd."

"Good. Now my assistants and I will take you to meet your new partners."

43

Marshall wished he'd never signed up for the auditions for the musical. There were a couple of dozen guys and half that many girls in the gym waiting their turn to sing. Some were singing quietly and others were talking in small groups. They'd each been given sheet music for God Bless America, the audition song. His stomach felt unsettled and his knees seemed wobbly.

The play director walked in and had them all sit in the chairs in front of the stage and then he called out a name and that person went up on stage. There was a piano player who gave the singer the first note and then he sang the song.

"Thank you, next is Paul Dobson," he said.

Ten singers had already tried out when Marshall's name was called. He took a deep breath and walked to the middle of the stage.

"Holy shit what the heck am I doing up here?" he thought.

The piano player gave him the note and he began singing the song. When it was over the director nodded. "Very nice, next is Katy Rego."

"Good job," one of his friends said as he walked past him.

"Was it okay?"

"I didn't know a dope like you could sing like that."

Marshall grinned. "Thanks... I think."

There were three corporals who worked for Sergeant Shepherd and each of them read a name off a list and the new dog handlers went with them to meet their dogs. Sergeant Shepherd took one handler also. Soon the corporals came back and read another name and took that handler to meet his dog. There were only three new handlers left when Sergeant Shepherd called Ethan's name.

"Follow me Randall," he said.

There were many rows of kennels with about 15 kennels in

each row. The Sergeant led Ethan to the 7th row and turned down it. On each side of the cement runway there were dogs in kennels watching them go past. Some barked and some just sat and watched them. A few of the kennels were empty, the dogs already out in the exercise field with their new handlers.

"So you're the guy getting Russell," the Sergeant said.

"So they tell me Sarge," Ethan said.

The Sergeant stopped and turned. "This is an exceptional dog Randall. In 18 years of working with military dogs I've only seen a handful that compare with this animal. He's as smart as they come and has a nose like few others. He needs a soft hand though. Goldens are not big bully dogs. You need to know that right up front."

"I understand," Ethan said.

"Have you had a dog all your life?"

"No Sarge, actually I haven't. My neighbor and best friend had a dog that I've grown up with. I read a book about these dogs and thought how it would be an amazing thing to work with one of them. That's why I applied for the job. Then when I mastered basic Arabic it seemed to seal my fate. They want me to use the dog not only for sniffing out explosives but also as a kind of good will ambassador."

"Muslims aren't really much into dogs, especially the older ones. They think they're un-clean. I think what the big brass is going for here is that you might be able to befriend some of the kids and younger men with the dog and your Arabic. That could prove to be a good way to gather some intelligence that you'd not otherwise be privy to. Ah, here we are."

Ethan stopped and looked into the kennel. The dog was a beauty. He was sitting just back from the door looking up. He looked like he was smiling.

"He's smiling at me," Ethan said.

"He is a very friendly guy," Sergeant Shepherd said.

He opened the door and the dog sat there smiling. Shepherd

nodded to Ethan.

"Call him by name."

Ethan squatted down and said, "Hey Russell."

The dog's tail began sweeping back and forth over the cement. He stood up and stepped forward and sat down right in front of Ethan. Then he raised his right paw.

"Oh my gosh," Ethan said, "He wants to shake hands."

Sergeant Shepherd was grinning from ear to ear. "I told you."

Ethan took the dog's paw in his hand and shook with him. Then he put his hands on either side of the handsome face and rubbed his ears. The dog put his face down and Ethan kissed him on top of the head.

"Hello my new friend," he whispered to the dog.

The dog surged forward and ended up knocking Ethan onto his butt. He put his arms around the dog and petted him while the Sergeant watched.

"I think he approves of you Randall," he said.

"Gosh he's beautiful," Ethan said.

He looked at the dog. He was a honey blond color, with long silky hair and well muscled legs and a full chest that looked very powerful. His tongue was hanging out the side of his mouth and he began lapping at Ethan's face. Ethan didn't mind a bit.

"I think you two will be just fine," Sergeant Shepherd said. "I'm going back to the office. Here is a leash, hook him up when you're done getting to know each other and take him out for a walk in the yard."

Ethan was still sitting on the floor. "So Russell, how about we go for a walk?"

The dog began to jump up and down.

"I'll take that as a yes," Ethan said.

He clipped the leash on the dog's collar and he fell right into step at his left side. Ethan and the dog walked out into the yard with the rest of the new handlers. Every one was smiling.

44

R ussell was the only golden retriever in the enclosure. The others were German Shepherds, Belgian Malinois, and two black labs. Each handler was just getting to know his partner and there were a lot of happy dogs and soldiers.

After half an hour Sarge Shepherd entered the enclosure and had them line up with their dogs on the left of each handler. He instructed the handlers to command their dogs to sit and they all did as told.

"You are about to embark on a remarkable mission in your military careers. You will be one of a very few soldiers who will be paired with a military dog. The only other occupation in the military that compares with you in small numbers is the sniper.

"Your dog has put in hundreds of hours with professional dog trainers. They are proficient in many duties. You will need to learn the commands and learn your dog's qualities and failings. They are not machines so they do have times when they will not do a prefect job. It will be your job to make them as close to perfect as possible.

"A human being has about 40 million olfactory receptors in their nose. These receptors allow you to smell everything from perfume to farts but nothing in extremely small quantities. These dogs have 2 Billion olfactory receptors. They can smell as little as .025 grams of a substance that they have been trained to seek out. There are 31 grams in an ounce, so you can imagine what a small amount .025 grams is.

"The dogs can clear as much area in a day looking for bad things as a man can do in one month. They are amazing animals and are very expensive to train. Each animal is worth about $80,000 in training time.

"Some of the things you will be looking for when in combat are ammonium nitrate, a bomb making chemical, detonator cord, KCL, nitrocellulose, C-4, RDX and a few other chemicals. These dogs can detect these things and will be actively looking for them when you give the command "Find Bad Things".

"If there is an emergency you can command "Seek, seek, seek." And they will work even more quickly.

"You will learn their commands and spend time with them for the next 12 weeks after which you and your partner will be deployed to somewhere in the world where your skills are needed.

"Discipline is essential and your dog is trained well. But there may be times you will need to be stern with them when a circumstance demands it. There is a difference between being stern and being harsh. Punishment must be carefully done and you will not strike your animal under any circumstances. Your dog is a soldier and will be at least one rank above you. Consequently if you strike a superior officer you will be court-marshaled. Are there any questions?"

"Are we allowed to give them treats?" one soldier asked. There were a few giggles from some of the men.

"You will treat them as you would a human partner. These are dogs after all. They love treats, they love being petted and they love to play games such as fetch. We have a good supply of tennis balls and you are encouraged to take some so you can play fetch with your dog while in downtime. They are like any other dog when it comes to eating also. You will be supplied with dog food but like any other dog these animals love bacon and weenies, and cheese doodles. When you are deployed in some third world country looking for explosives you will probably share your meals with your dog. That is fine as long as you make sure he or she gets plenty to eat and drink. Their health is up to you. There are military veterinarians that will be on hand to treat them if needed but you are their handler and you must take care of them. "

"Should we let civilians touch them?"

"That depends on the situation. If you are doing crowd

control or manning a check post where you are trying to keep the peace it's best to have the dog look menacing and keep people away. If you are just out mingling and some kid comes up and wants to pet your dog, no problem. I'm sure Randall here will get a lot more requests for petting with his golden than you guys with the Belgians will get. That golden is much more friendly looking than those black faced toothy little guys. It is up to you to make sure that anyone approaching the dog is not going to harm him."

Ethan looked down at Russell and the dog looked up and grinned at him.

"Dang, I think he understands English," Ethan thought to himself.

"Ok it's time to put your dog back in his kennel. You'll need to feed them and water them and then take them for a toilet run and the day is over for them. We'll resume tomorrow at 0800."

Ethan led Russell into the kennel and filled his dish with dog food. He filled his water bowl with fresh water, swept down the floor and cleaned up some crap. Russell was finished with his food so Ethan took him out to an area for toilet duty. He didn't know for sure how to make him go but noticed another handler nearby.

"Toilet Brady," he said.

The dog lifted his leg against the fence and peed. Then he sniffed the ground in a few places, spun around a couple of times and hunched up and crapped.

"They know to do that too?" Ethan asked in awe.

"Smartest damn dogs I've ever seen," the other guy said.

"Russell, toilet."

Russell began sniffing for the correct spot. He found it a minute later, hunched up, pooped and then turned around and lifted his leg and peed on the poop pile. Then he looked up at Ethan and smiled.

"Damn!" Ethan said.

45

Marshall was sweating bullets. He looked over his shoulder and put the car into reverse and then began backing up.

"Wait until you see the back window post and then begin turning," he said in his mind.

He saw the window post of the car parked next to the curb and turned the wheel so the rear end of the car began moving into the open spot between two cars that were parked. He gave the car a little gas and is slipped into the slot. Then he turned the wheel back to the other side to straighten the car out. He felt the rear tire skim against the curb.

"Oh crap!" he said to himself.

The car straightened out and he moved back until he was very close to the rear car. Then he braked and put the car in drive and moved it forward so it was centered in the spot.

The Driver's License guy jotted something on his clipboard and said, "Okay now pull out into traffic."

Marshall looked over his left shoulder and pulled out.

"Make a left at the light."

It was a One-Way street so Marshall turned onto it and stayed in the outside lane.

"Change lanes and turn left."

Marshall looked over his shoulder and changed lanes and turned left at the corner.

The instructor wrote again on his clipboard.

When they'd arrived back at the Licensing Station the man wrote a few more notes and seemed to be adding some things up.

"Your parallel parking was right on," he said. "I took one point off because you crowd the crosswalks a bit. Otherwise you did well."

"So I passed?"

"You passed."

Later he was waiting online with Skype booted up for Ethan to contact him. They tried to talk every couple of days but sometimes Ethan couldn't get away so Marshall waited to see if he'd appear. There was a beep and Ethan appeared on his screen.

"Hey pal, how you doing?" Ethan said smiling.

"Hi jeez it's good to see you."

"What's new at home?"

"I got my driver's license today."

"Oh man, I'll have to tell everyone to stay off the streets."

Marshall laughed. "Yeah, and the sidewalk too."

"That's good Marshall. Now when I get home you can drive me around."

"I'll do it. Anything new with you?"

"I got my dog."

"No kidding, one of those Shepherds?"

Ethan laughed. "No they gave me a golden retriever."

"They're not very scary," Marshall said.

"I'm not suppose to scare people with it. With my being able to speak passable Arabic they want me to kind of be a good will ambassador as well as a bomb sniffing dog handler. They think I might be able to befriend some of the locals and get some intel."

"What's his name?"

"Russell. He's the smartest dog I've ever seen. I've been working with him for only a few days but I can see already that he's an amazing dog."

"Are you worried about being a bomb finder?"

"Well with Russell at my side I'll know where the bombs are so I think I'll be safer than most of the other guys. All Russell and I do is find the bomb. Then bomb guys come and make it safe. They have the dangerous job."

"Well, I'm glad to hear that you're not messing with them," Marshall said.

"This dog can smell like you wouldn't believe. I'll give you an example. When a person comes into a room and there is spaghetti sauce on the stove he smells spaghetti sauce. When a dog comes into the room he smells, tomatoes, garlic, onions, oregano, Parmesan cheese and anything else in spaghetti sauce. His nose is thousands of times more sensitive than a human's nose. They can find tiny amounts of explosives. So I think I'm going to be fairly safe."

"I wonder what a fart smells like to him?" Marshall said.

Ethan broke out laughing. "Only you would ask that."

"I got a part in the play," Marshall said.

"No kidding? Which part did you get?"

"Marius."

"No way! He's one of the main characters. You're going to be Marius?"

Marshall nodded. "I've got a lot of stuff to learn. I hope I don't screw it up and ruin the whole show."

"You'll do great. I'm real proud of you. I sure wish I could see it when they perform it."

"Any idea when you might be coming home?"

"This is a 12 week course. In a couple more weeks we'll be moving into new quarters and our dogs will live with us like they do on duty someplace. Once we've spent a few weeks with them they give us a leave to go home. I'll be bringing Russell with me. It gets them used to traveling with their handler."

"Cool, so maybe in a few weeks?"

Ethan nodded. "I'd guess it might be a couple of months from now. I'll let you know."

"The play is going to be in 9 weeks and we're going to do it 4 times. We start on a Thursday, then do it again Friday, Saturday and Sunday afternoon."

"It'd be cool if I could get there for it. I'll sure try."

They talked for a bit longer and then Ethan had to go.

"I'll talk to you in a couple of days," he said.

"I'll be here. It's so good to see you Ethan," Marshall said with a lump in his throat. "I love you Ethan."

"Same here pal. Hang in there I'll see you in person soon."

Ethan clicked off and Marshall sat there looking at the blank screen. The past months had been tough. He'd never spent that much time without Ethan being around. He was busy in school thankfully so that made the time pass a little faster. He wasn't sure how he was going to get past the time Ethan spent deployed overseas. He dreaded thinking about it.

46

Every day Ethan worked with Russell he got closer to the dog and was amazed at his intelligence and stamina. They would run obstacle courses, sniff different "bad things", take down "bad people", and then they'd have playtime.

They were encouraged to reward the dog with a game of fetch rather than an edible treat. A tennis ball was a much easier thing to have in your pocket than a messy dog-treat. Plus it seemed that the fun time was just as much appreciated as a food treat by the dog.

Once they were through the initial training weeks with their dogs each handler moved into a barracks that consisted of small rooms for each of them. Their dogs moved in with them. This was done so the dog would get used to being with their handler day and night and look to them as their friend and boss. It was also done so they would get used to living with humans, which was something they'd be forced to do when deployed into a war zone. There were no special kennels in places like Afghanistan for the dogs. They were treated like any other soldier.

Russell and Ethan became like one. The dog was at his side during the day while they trained and at night he slept on the floor on a mat by his bed. Ethan even allowed the dog to follow him to the shower once a week for a bath. He had a bottle of dog shampoo, which he used to lather him up. Then he lathered his own hair and body up and they rinsed off together. The dog loved it.

One night just as they were bedding down for the night Russell sat up and listened with his head cocked to the side. He could hear something that Ethan couldn't hear.

"What's wrong boy?"

The dog looked at him and had a look of concern on his face.

"What do you hear?" Ethan said listening carefully.

Russell whined and put his face in Ethan's lap. He seemed

uncomfortable about something.

Then Ethan heard it off in the distance. There was a low rumble of thunder.

"It's just a thunder storm kiddo, it won't hurt you."

The dog stuck right to him as close as he could get.

Ethan turned out the light and lay down. Russell laid his head on the edge of the bed and sat there looking at Ethan.

"Lay down boy, you're okay."

The storm got louder and the wind began to blow. Russell began to whine and pant. Ethan put his hand on the back of his neck and petted him.

"It's okay Russell, it's a storm. It won't hurt you."

The dog got up and put his front paws on Ethan's bed. He put his face next to Ethan's chest. Ethan stroked his silky fur.

"Okay, come up here," he said.

The dog jumped up and snuggled next to him. He was still shivering and panting but seemed less afraid. Ethan put his arm around the dog and pulled him close.

"I'll protect you boy," he whispered.

Outside the storm rumbled and the wind blew. Rain came in hard driving sheets against the corrugated steel roof of the barracks. Ethan noticed Russell had calmed down a little but was concerned. If he was this afraid of a storm, what would happen if they got into a fire-fight in a war zone and there were guns going off all over the place? He had a hard time getting to sleep thinking about it.

Ethan woke to a wet tongue slurping his face. He opened his eyes and there was Russell with his golden retriever grin looking at him.

"Hey boy, are you okay now?" he said.

The dog's tail hammered on the bed.

"You gotta go out?"

The dog jumped up and started jumping up and down. Ethan got out of the bed and slipped on his gym shorts and a tee shirt. He walked barefoot to the back fenced-in area where the dogs could go to the toilet. Russell watered the fence three times and then sniffed for a minute until he found the right spot. He hunched up and circled three times and then dropped a turd on the grass. Then he ran back happily to his master.

"Good boy," Ethan said ruffling his ears. But in his mind Ethan was worried. He knew he had to talk to Sarge Shepherd. He was afraid that it might mean an end to him and Russell being partners and he didn't want to do it. But he knew he must for his sake and the dog's sake.

After breakfast he knocked on the office door.

"Enter," Sarge Shepherd said.

Ethan walked in and stood at attention.

"Sarge, I would like a word with you," he said.

"Sit Randall. What seems to be the problem?"

Ethan told the Sarge about how Russell acted when the storm came through the previous night. Sarge Shepherd listened and then looked concerned.

"Do you think he might be afraid of loud noises or gunfire?"

"I don't know Sarge. We haven't done any drills with loud noise but the thunder sure spooked him. I hated to come to you about it but I know it's important for him not to be gun shy. That would be a bad deal for everyone, especially Russell."

The Sergeant opened a file cabinet and dug through it until he found Russell's file. He read through it and his forehead frowned.

"Hmm, there is something here that we might have missed," he said.

"Sarge?"

"There is a paragraph about him when he was a pup. It seems a summer storm came through and he was lying sleeping and didn't pay attention to it at all. Then a gust of wind came through an open window and blew vase of plastic flowers that was sitting on the kitchen table off the table and it fell right on his head. It scared him but didn't hurt him. Then a few days later another storm blew in and he got the heck out of the kitchen and lay down in the living room. He'd just closed his eyes and another gust blew a lamp off a table and it also landed on him. That time he ran and hid under the bed."

"Oh no, twice in a row."

"Yup, and from then on when it began thundering in the west, he headed for the bedroom and hid until it was past."

"Holy cow, what do you think?" Ethan asked.

"I think we need to see if he's gun shy."

Ethan nodded. His heart was thumping in his chest. This could ruin everything.

47

"Let's take him out to the drill field and see what happens when we fire a weapon," Sarge said.

Ethan went and got Russell from the room and they went to one of the empty drill fields.

"I'll walk off here a little way and you have some happy time with him. Throw his ball a few times and once he gets going I'll fire my weapon. If he bolts we'll know it's not going to be his job in life to be a military dog. If not I'll move in closer and fire again."

"Okay," Ethan said.

They walked apart and Ethan produced the ball. The dog jumped up and down and was very excited about playing ball. Ethan threw the ball out into the field and Russell ran as fast as he could go and picked it up and returned it. He dropped it at Ethan's feet and sat waiting for another toss. Ethan threw it a second time and Russell retrieved it. When he threw it the third time Sarge fired his gun. Russell looked over at him but kept right on speeding toward the ball. Sarge walked twenty feet closer and the next time Ethan threw the ball he fired just as soon as it left Ethan's hand. Russell glanced at him but took right off after the ball.

Sarge was grinning as he walked up to Ethan.

"Well, I don't think it's the loud noise that bothers him. I think it's the thunder which I agree is a loud noise but much different than gunfire.

"So do you think he's okay?" Ethan asked.

"I think he's fine. It doesn't rain much in the Middle East and they hardy ever have a big thunder storm so I wouldn't worry about him."

Ethan was glad to hear that. He knelt and hugged the dog. Russell licked his face and dropped the ball waiting for another toss.

The final weeks of training went well. Ethan and Russell were a real team and they worked well together. Russell could find many different "bad things" and Ethan trusted his nose completely.

Ethan was promoted to corporal and Russell was promoted to Staff Sergeant, two ranks higher than Ethan. He was outfitted with a vest that he wore under his harness with his rank and the Marine insignia on it.

"I'll be at the airport around noon," Ethan said to his mom. "Marshall told me he had one more performance of the play tomorrow afternoon, I'd like to surprise him and go to it if I get home on time."

"Oh honey, he's so good in it. He really steals the show. I had no idea that little prankster could sing so wonderfully."

"Marshall's a smart talented kid. I think since he was in my shadow so much it just never came out of him."

"Well he's done an outstanding job in this play."

"Don't tell him I'm coming... and Mom, I'm bringing my partner home with me."

"The dog?"

"Yup, and he outranks me so you have to be nice to him."

His mom laughed and promised to be on her best behavior.

Military dogs are allowed on all flights and are not required to be in a travel cage like regular dogs. Their training gives them that privilege and the airlines are glad to have them aboard.

When Ethan and Russell got on the plane everyone watched and smiled at them. Many complimented Ethan on how beautiful his dog was. He took his seat and Russell lay down on the floor between his feet. It was cramped but he only had enough money for one ticket.

Soon a hostess came to them and told him they had an empty seat that he could move to and that they had one for Russell too. He followed her up to the front of the plane and was surprised when she pointed to two seats in first class. They were like big recliners.

"This will be more comfortable for you," she said smiling.

"Thank you very much," he said.

"No, thank you very much."

Russell looked around and gave everyone his golden retriever grin. They all seemed very glad to have him aboard.

Once they'd taken off Russell looked out the window next to Ethan.

"Is he afraid of heights?" a lady on the other side asked.

"No he's just curious," Ethan said. "Dogs don't have a sense of height. These dogs are trained to parachute with their trainers and it doesn't bother them a bit. They think it's fun."

"He's beautiful," she said.

"Thank you ma-am. He's a great partner."

"Are you going... over there?"

"We're going home for two weeks and then we're going to Afghanistan."

"Oh dear. I'll pray for you young man," she said.

"Thank you ma-am."

Russell settled down and took a nap. Ethan read a book he'd brought along and a while later a little boy about ten stopped by them.

"Can I pet your dog?" he asked.

Russell woke up and licked the kid's face. He giggled.

"Sure, his name is Russell," Ethan said.

"Hello Russell," the kid said. He stroked the dog's coat and Russell enjoyed the attention. "Are you looking for drugs?" the kid asked.

"No Russell is a military dog. He's a Staff Sergeant in rank. He sniffs explosives."

"Like bombs?"

"Yeah, bombs and things like that."

The kid thought about it for a minute. "Is that dangerous?

"As long as I have Russell with me, I don't have to worry

about stepping on a bomb or a land mine. So I guess I'm pretty safe."

The kid digested that. Then he smiled. "Thank you for letting me pet him."

Then he hugged Russell and the dog lapped his face. "You're a good boy," he said. "You go find those bombs and be careful," he said.

Ethan watched him go back to his mother and smiled. He was pretty proud of being a Marine and making it into this small number of soldiers and dogs that did such an important job. Russell looked at him and grinned.

"Yeah, you ARE a good boy," he said ruffling his ears.

They landed about half an hour later and many of the people on the plane told him to be safe and careful as they filed off the plane. He went and found his duffle bag and headed out to the waiting area. He was looking for his parents. His dad walked up behind him and slapped him on the back.

"Hey soldier what's up?"

Ethan looked around and there was his dad grinning from ear to ear.

"Hey Dad," he said. They embraced and he could tell his dad was very emotional. He stepped back and looked at his son in his uniform and tears came to his eyes.

"I'm so proud of you," he said.

Then his mom came running up and hugged him. She was weeping too.

Finally they let go and Ethan said, "Hey I want you to meet my partner."

"This is Russell."

They looked down at the dog and he was grinning. He held up his paw to shake.

"Hello Russell," his dad said.

"Did you teach him that?"

"He knew it before I knew him. He's a pretty smart guy."

"He's almost as handsome as Buzzie, next door."

Ethan laughed. "Yeah okay. Am I going to be in time to catch the play?"

"If we get going you should be home in time to see most of it. Marshall doesn't know you're coming so he'll really be surprised.

They went to the parking lot and loaded up and headed for home. Russell watched out the window and was very interested in everything.

48

Marshall's parents very happy to see Ethan and they were happy to meet Russell, everyone except Buzzy. Marshall's dad brought him to Ethan's parents back yard where they were listening to Ethan tell of his training and he looked at the big dog and sat down. Russell walked over to him and he got up and walked away.

His dad was watching and grinned at Ethan.

"He's jealous," he said.

Ethan nodded. By now he'd changed into shorts and a Marines tee shirt. He walked over to where Buzzie was sitting on the edge of the patio and squatted down by him.

"Hey Buzzie, aren't you glad to see me?"

The dog looked up at him and his little stub tail wiggled.

"You know we're still best friends. That new dog works with me at my job, I think if you got to know him you'd like him."

Buzzie had no idea what he was talking about but knew that his old friend Ethan was making up to him. He got up and pushed into Ethan's lap. Ethan petted the dog and made a big fuss about him.

"Come on," he said, and he carried him over to where Russell was watching them.

He put Buzzie down and the two dogs sniffed each other. Buzzie went around back and sniffed Russell's rear end. Then it seemed like all was well. The two dogs began to play.

"Well, that's good," Ethan said.

"If you want to see the play you'd better get going," his dad said.

Ethan drove his pickup to the school and when he went to the ticket booth the lady told him to go on in. He snuck into the theater and stood in the back watching the play.

Marshall was on stage with the other students who were planning on a revolution. Soon the song, *Do You Hear the People*

Sing? was sung and he smiled as Marshall sang with gusto. He slipped into a seat and watched as the play continued.

In the last act Marshall's character had a solo *Empty Chairs and Empty Tables* where he sang of his lost friends who'd died in the revolution. He was just about to the end and he spotted Ethan sitting in the last row. Ethan knew that Marshall had seen him but the kid kept on singing and finished the song beautifully. As the audience applauded he looked Ethan and smiled.

After the finale, the cast took their bows and Marshall came running down the aisle from the stage. Ethan was standing in the aisle and Marshall ran into his arms and they hugged hard and long.

Ethan could feel Marshall sobbing. "Hey don't cry."

"I'm sorry, I'm just so happy to see you. Why didn't you tell me you were coming?"

"I wanted to surprise you."

"Well you sure as heck did that," Marshall said.

People were walking by and nearly everyone complimented Marshall on his singing and acting. Ethan smiled all the while.

"So you're quite the singer now," he said.

"Oh jeez. It's nothing compared to what you do."

"Let me tell you Marshall, I'd rather face ten bombs than get up in front of all these people and sing by my self."

"Really?"

"Really. Now go get changed. We're having a cookout and we need to see if Buzzie has killed Russell yet."

"He came with you?"

Ethan nodded.

"Cool! Be right back."

Many of Ethan's friends showed up during the evening and they had a grand time. It was well after midnight when everyone finally left. The parents were all in bed. The only ones left by the firepit were Ethan and Marshall and the dogs.

Ethan sat down on an outdoor couch next to Marshall and

put his arm around the younger boy. Marshall leaned into him.

"Finally... we can talk together," he said.

"Yeah," Marshall said.

"So how's it been with me gone?"

"Lonely at first but I've been busy with senior classes and driving class so the time went pretty fast. The play kept me really busy. That was a heck of a good idea you had for me to try out. I didn't expect to get such a big part though. So I've been keeping busy but I do miss you though. When you get used to being with someone every day it's hard not to have them there."

"I know, it was the same for me. Many times I wished I could sit and talk with you about things."

They sat quietly for a while. Russell and Buzzie were lying next to each other on the patio floor.

"He's a beautiful dog," Marshall said.

"He's almost human," Ethan said, "there isn't a day that goes by that I'm not amazed at something he does."

"He's a bomb dog... isn't that dangerous?"

"I'm probably the last person in the squad who has a chance of stepping on a bomb. Russell can find a speck of explosives in a pile of rubble. I'm not very worried."

"I'll worry enough for both of us," Marshall said.

Ethan hugged him. "Just keep us in your prayers," he said.

They got up and hugged goodnight and went to their own bedrooms. Marshall looked out the window, as Ethan got ready for bed. Russell was there waiting and watching his master. Ethan slipped off his shorts and shirt and turned out the light. Marshall could see the dog jump up onto the bed with Ethan.

"Come on Buzzie," he said patting the bed. The dog jumped up and rooted around until he had a nest made in the blankets. Then he lay down and in no time he was snoring.

Marshall looked at the little dog. "You aren't quite as pretty as Russell but you're a pretty good boy," he said.

He patted the dog and in no time he fell asleep.

49

The two-week leave went by fast. Ethan and Marshall and the dogs did a lot of fun stuff during the time. They camped for a couple of nights at a nearby lake, swam, fished and cooked over a wood fire. They spent a day at a water-park and the rest of the time they spent with their families. The dogs became great friends.

It was funny to watch when they'd throw a tennis ball for them. Russell galloped out to fetch with long graceful strides and Buzzie ran like he was possessed to get there with him. Russell always waited for Buzzie to get his ball and then they raced back.

Ethan was on the phone when Marshall walked into his bedroom.

"Okay, thank you," he said.

"What's up?"

"I was checking on my plane ticket. I wanted to be sure they knew Russell was going to be with me."

Marshall felt his stomach drop.

"I kinda forgot it's tomorrow you have to leave," he said.

"I have my duty now Marshall, it's my job."

"Do you know where you'll go?"

Ethan nodded. "I'm going to Afghanistan."

"Oh jeez," Marshall said.

"Marshall I'll be okay. The squad is trained to the max. We know what we're doing and with Russell I'll be safe as can be."

Marshall put his arms around his friend. "I know," he said.

They had one last cookout that evening and the next morning Marshall drove them to the airport. He carried Ethan's duffel to the gate and he checked in. They'd already upgraded him to business class so Russell could have his own seat.

"Well, I gotta go through the inspection," he said.

Marshall nodded. He hugged Ethan hard and his eyes filled with tears.

"You promise you'll come back," he said.

"I promise Marshall, I promise."

They broke their hug and Ethan turned and led Russell through the security check. They got on an escalator and rode up one flight. Just as he got to the door to his gate he stopped and turned and smiled at Marshall and then walked out of sight.

Marshall hurried out of the terminal and got to the car. He shut the door and put his head down and cried...for a long time.

He sat and waited until Ethan's plane had taxied to the runway and then watched as it picked up speed and rose off the tarmac. He followed it until he could see it no more in the sky.

Then he started the car and drove home. His heart felt like it was empty.

50

The first thing that struck Ethan about Afghanistan was how unbelievably hot it was. He and his squad filed off the military transport plane and lined up on the tarmac. He and Russell and one other dog and handler were a part of a squad of thirty Marines. They were ready for whatever came up. They checked in with the local commander and were transported by truck forty miles north to the post they would work from for the next many months.

"What the hale would ennybuddy fight over this place for?" one of the southern guys said.

"Aint's worth spit," another said.

"It'd make a good gravel quarry. We could gravel the whole fricking world."

They chattered and laughed as they drove through little hamlets along the way. There were few women to be seen but there were lots of kids along the road begging for candy and cigarettes.

A few old men watched them. Some looked friendly but many looked angry.

They got to their base and unloaded. It was a collection of stone buildings that had a new stone fence built around it. The fence was about five feet high and was topped with razor wire. There were gun towers every twenty feet on the outside perimeter. It looked like it had been built in the fifteenth century.

"Home sweet home," one of the guys said.

"Randall, you and Stewart and your dogs get the bridal suite," their Sergeant said.

Ethan grinned. "Yes Sergeant."

He and the other handler led their dogs to the building he'd pointed out to them. It was a small hut with a dirt floor and two bunks. There were two windows with no glass in them and the door was a blanket hung from the top of the door opening."

"Lovely, I wonder where the hot-tub is," Toby Stewart said.

"At least we have beds," Ethan said poking the lumpy mattress.

"If you can call that a bed. We better spray them with disinfectant.

They stowed their gear and fed and watered their dogs. Stewart had a German shepherd named Thor.

Toby Stewart was from Montana and a prefect example of an American farm boy. He was a big guy with a wide easy smile and was always ready to lend a hand to anyone. He had been paired with a German shepherd that weighed-in at a bit over a hundred and ten pounds. Thor looked fierce and acted the part when he was on duty. When off duty he was a happy friendly dog that loved to be petted and loved to play ball. He and Russell got along well and had many play-fighting matches after which they'd lie down next to each other for a nap.

There was a large tent that was the mess hall, several buildings that served as barracks and an outhouse. It was like living in the stone-ages.

They were all settled in when the Sergeant came and asked Ethan to go with him to meet the local tribal leader. They walked to a hut near the center of the little village and there were several grizzled old men sitting on the ground sipping coffee from little cups. They sat with them and were offered some coffee. Ethan sipped it and nearly spit. It was so strong he thought he might have to chew it.

"Shukran jazkan," "Thank you very much," he said.

The old man who seemed to be in charge nodded his head.

"Ahcan," "Welcome," he said.

"Hasan kalb?" "Good dog?" another old man asked.

Ethan nodded. *"Rahia,"* "Smells," Ethan said.

The old man nodded. Then he summoned a kid who looked to be about 12 who stood nearby. The boy was wearing one of the typical long dirty-white shirts, was barefoot and grinning from ear to ear. He had black hair that surrounded his head in curls and dark eyes. He had a wide smile with white even teeth that made him a pretty cute kid.

"*Jalal,*" the old man said.

"*Salaam,*" Jalal said. "I speak your English language," he said smiling brightly.

"Hello Jalal, I am Ethan and this is my dog Russell."

The kid spoke to the elders in Arabic.

They nodded their heads.

"Ru-sell and Eee than," the old man said.

Ethan nodded and smiled.

Jalal looked pleased with himself.

"I will be your interpreter yes?"

"I think that would be fine. I will have to ask my boss."

"I understand. Here this man is boss."

"Please tell him we are here to help and to keep them safe. We will do all we can to help your country."

Jalal began rattling the translation and he heard "Eee than" in the mix. When he had finished the old man nodded and took Ethan's hand and shook with him.

"*Shukran,*" "Thank you," he said.

Ethan nodded and got up. Jalal went with him.

"So how do you know English?" he asked the kid.

"When I was little the soldiers took me in. My family was killed by a Taliban road-bomb as my father pushed our cart to the market to sell our turnips that we grew on our farm. All others were killed but I survived because of your good doctors." He raised his shirt and showed Ethan a scar on his thigh. The scar ran almost the entire length of the thigh and looked like it had been sliced open by shrapnel.

"The soldiers decided to learn me the English and I am a very smart boy," he said, his teeth flashing a big grin.

"Well, I am very glad that you are here. It will make my job much easier. I can speak some Arabic but not as well as you speak English."

"I am a valuable man," the kid said.

"Yes you are," Ethan replied grinning.

They got to Ethan's hut and the kid followed him inside.

"So where do I sleep?" he asked.

Ethan looked surprised. "You don't have a place to sleep?"

"If no one gives me a place I sleep with the goats and sheep in the village. But I would much more like to sleep in here with you and Ru-sell. The Taliban do not like boys who are friendly with the soldiers so I must be careful. A few weeks ago, one of my friends, who also knew the English was killed by the Taliban because he helped the American soldiers. They found him beheaded."

Ethan's stomach turned. How could these people do something like that to a kid?

"Well I guess if it's okay with my roommate and our commander, you can stay here."

Jalal nodded. "We will be much good friends. Jalal will help you to find the bad guys."

51

Ethan talked to his commanding officer and Toby Stewart and they both were fine with Jalal staying with them. There wasn't room for another bed but the military provided large cushions for their working dogs and the supply Sergeant had a whole stack of them in the supply building. He got a couple of new ones for Jalal. Both Russell and Thor usually slept on the bare floor or on the bed with their partner so they wouldn't mind.

Jalal was very happy with the nice soft cushions.

"They are much good compared to a stinky goat and a pile of straw," he said as he tried them out.

Corporal Stewart and Thor came back from a look around a bit later and Jalal was very interested in the big dog. He was a little hesitant with him.

"Thor is *"Da ha mea kalb?"* "Attack dog?" he asked.

"He is bomb dog and can be attack dog too," Ethan said.

"Ru-sell, bomb dog but *"Lateef"* "Nice," he said.

Ethan nodded. "Too pretty," he said.

"Yes make bad men not afraid like Thor."

Thor heard his name and walked up to the kid. Jalal put his hand out tentatively and the big dog licked it. He broke out in a huge smile.

"Thor likes Jalal. This will be a good place for me to live with two such wonderful dogs and two soldiers to protect me. No more stinky goats for Jalal."

They went to the mess tent and took Jalal along with them. They introduced him to the other guys and told everyone he was their interpreter and to be good to him. They all seemed to be glad to see the kid. It kind of reminded them of home to have a kid around.

Jalal ate like a typical teenager. He shoveled food into his mouth until there was nothing left to eat. He was grinning from ear to ear.

"You Americans have much good food. Jalal likes hamburg and such things. Here we eat goat and beans and such. Not good like your food. Beans make me make big stink too."

They all laughed when he said that.

"We'll tell the cook not to make beans then," Ethan said.

They went back to their hut and Ethan and Toby took turns going to he shower tent. There wasn't a lot of extra water but there was enough for them to have a shower every few days. They came back and were dressed in gym shorts and tank tops.

"Is that the only clothes you have?" Ethan asked Jalal.

"Yes, I am very poor."

"I'll give you one of my long tee shirts and you go and take a shower and we'll wash your clothes while you wash up. Then you can sit in the tee shirt until it your clothes are dry. That way you'll have something clean to wear."

Jalal was all for that idea.

"I have made shower before. It is most wonderful thing. Here I must wash from a pail or by the stream that is below the mountains. There the water is very cold."

Ethan handed him a clean tee shirt. It was long enough to keep him covered while his long shirt dried. Jalal pulled his shirt off and wrapped a towel around his waist and went to the shower. Ethan took his long shirt out to the supply tent and got a bucket and some water and soap and washed the shirt. Then he hung it over a tent rope to dry.

"Did you see the scars on his back?" Stewart asked when he came back.

"No, do you mean Jalal?"

Stewart nodded. "His back looks like he's been beaten."

Ethan shook his head. "I'll ask him."

Soon Jalal came back with a wide smile. His hair was all wet and wild looking but he looked very happy.

"Jalal no longer smells like the goat," he said grinning. "This is good yes?"

Ethan nodded. "Yes it is not good to smell like a goat. Your shirt is drying. You can keep that tee shirt if you like it."

"Jalal likes the tee shirt. I look like American yes?"

Ethan and Stewart laughed. "Well, usually Americans wear a bit more than a tee shirt."

The shirt was long enough that it covered Jalal nearly to his knees. He beamed as he sat on his bed and the two dogs came to him. He petted them and talked to them.

"Jalal, Toby said you have scars on your back. How did that happen?"

The kid looked up. "The bad men, the Taliban. Some of my friends and I were playing football, you know, the game you call soccer, and they said we were... is the word imitating?"

Ethan nodded.

"They said we were imitating the Americans and they took us and beat us. One boy was wearing a Chicago Cubs hat and they beat him so bad he nearly died. These are bad men Eee-than."

Ethan and Toby just sat and shook their heads. They knew this was a hellhole but had no idea of how horrible it really was.

"Well, we're going out on patrol at 0600 so we better get some sleep," Ethan said.

They all bedded down and the dogs lay by Jalal on his mat. He grinned up at the guys.

"The dogs they like Jalal. They will protect me."

"You're the safest boy in all of Afghanistan," Ethan said.

"Goodnight Jalal," the two soldiers said.

"Masank kheir."

52

They rolled out of their bunks at 0500 and got ready for a patrol. They put vests on the dogs that had armor plating in them just like the vests they wore under their outer jackets. Once they were all ready they walked to the mess hall for breakfast. Jalal was wearing his freshly laundered shirt and it looked pretty good.

He was very chatty and they went through the chow line and filled their plates. When they sat down one of the other guys looked at Jalal and then said to Ethan, "He knows what bacon is doesn't he?"

Ethan looked surprised. He'd forgotten that Muslims don't eat pork.

"Um Jalal, are you sure you want that meat? It's pig."

Jalal looked up and grinned. "I have learned that pig is very good. Please do not tell the elders that I have sinned. But to sin by eating bacon is worth the sin. It might even be worth a small beating."

He was grinning from ear to ear.

"Okey dokey," Ethan said.

"What is okey dokey?"

"It means everything is okay."

"Okey dokey," Jalal said.

The patrol was to check the road to the next village. There was a supply convoy coming from that village later in the day so they wanted to be sure there were no IED's planted on the road. The plan was for Ethan and Toby and their dogs to walk along either side of the road and let the dogs sniff. There were a dozen other squad members behind them to watch for bad guys and keep them safe while their dogs worked. Behind them was a truck to carry them all back once the road was cleared.

"You stay here," Ethan said.

"But Jalal can help," Jalal said.

"It's too dangerous. You have no armor and there is no need for an interpreter. We'll be back in a few hours. You stay here and see if you can help with any chores."

The boy nodded and petted the dogs.

"Be careful," he said to them.

Ethan had a knot in his stomach as they started along the rock-strewn road. It was barely a road, more like a track that had the biggest rocks cleared from the surface of it.

"Russell, seek," he said.

The dog began working along the right side of the road while Thor worked the left side. Their noses were going full speed and their two handlers were alert and watching for anything out of the ordinary.

They covered the first couple of miles without anything happening. Then Thor alerted. He stopped and sat down which meant he'd smelled one of the 'bad things".

"Dog alert!' Toby said.

He called Thor back and one of the bomb guys came up and got on his knees and began checking it out. He moved very carefully and soon picked up a piece of metal that looked like an old exploded shell casing.

"Just an old shell," he said. "All clear."

They started out again and were nearly to the other village when Ethan noticed a spot on the road where the earth looked fresh. He slowly walked to it and Russell immediately sat and indicated an alert.

"Dog alert," Ethan said.

He called Russell back. "Russell, out, out."

Russell backed up with him to a safe distance while the bomb guy looked it over. He took his knife and probed carefully into the soft ground and then pushed a couple of rocks aside.

"Got one," he said.

A second bomb guy came up and together they found the detonator and made the thing safe. Then they dug it from the road and carried it back to the truck and put it into an armored barrel.

"Good boy," Ethan said ruffling Russell's ears. The dog's tail wagged furiously.

They made it to the village and loaded onto the transport truck for the ride back to their base. It had been a productive morning and a good way to start their deployment in Afghanistan.

Jalal was waiting for them by the front gate and was all smiles as they unloaded.

"Did Ru-sell find any bomb?" he asked.

"Yea he found one," Ethan said.

Jalal knelt by the dog and hugged his neck. "You are *Hasan kalb*," "Good dog."

They went to their hut and got out of their combat gear and washed up.

"So... " Jalal said, "we will now have lunch?"

Ethan and Toby laughed. "A typical teenage boy," Toby said.

"Yup, a bottomless pit."

53

They settled into a routine and the time passed slowly. Some days they did nothing but maintain their gear and take turns watching the perimeter for intruders. Other days they went out on patrol and Ethan and Toby and the dogs did their thing. Over the next many weeks they found several IED's and disarmed them without incident.

Jalal was very popular around the camp. He was such an outgoing kid that everyone looked after him and enjoyed him. He still spent most of his time in the dog handler's hut.

"Jalal, I'm going to use the computer to contact my family today," Ethan said. "Would you like to come with me?"

"I know of computers but never operated one Eee-than."

"You can just watch. I think you'll enjoy it. I will be talking to my best friend too."

Jalal was excited about the idea of seeing people on the other side of the world but had no idea how that was possible.

Ethan had emailed Marshall to be on Skype at a certain time so they could talk. Of course Ethan was 8 hours ahead so it was the middle of the night where Marshall was at the same time.

He and Jalal waited for the connection; Jalal was fascinated.

"How does this little thing let you see the other side of the world?" he asked.

"This computer sends a signal to a satellite in the sky and that satellite bounces it to another and then to the computer in Marshall's bedroom. Then he can see us and we can see him."

Jalal nodded. "What is a satellite?"

Just then the screen opened and there was Marshall sitting at his computer table. He looked a little rough around the edges.

"Hey," he said.

"Hey," Ethan said. "Were you sleeping?"

Marshall nodded. "I fell asleep and just woke when my alarm went off a minute ago. Your parents and mine are on their way up to my room. How's it going?"

"It's going good. Russell has found a bunch of bombs and we've surely saved a bunch of lives and injuries. It's hot as hell here but otherwise I'm just fine."

"Good, oh wait here's your dad."

Ethan and his parents talked for a bit and then Marshall's parents chatted with him. They knew he had limited time so they signed off and let Marshall come back on.

"What's going on there?" Ethan asked.

"Graduation's next week. Then I guess I'm going to work at the hardware store for the summer. Then I don't know what I'll do. I'm accepted at the university but I don't know what I want to do yet."

"You'll figure it out. Take your time and find something that you'll be happy with all of your life."

Ethan pulled Jalal into the picture.

"Marshall this is Jalal. He's our go-to guy here."

Jalal looked a little hesitant.

"What do I say Eee-than?"

"Just say hello."

"HELLO!" he shouted.

Marshall laughed. "You don't have to shout, I can hear you. So are you keeping Ethan and Russell safe?"

"Yes, I am the guy who knows all that goes on here. I keep my ear to the ground, as they say. Eee-than is a good man."

Marshall smiled. "I know that. Ethan and I have been friends all of our lives. You watch out for him. I want him to come back here when he's done over there."

"I will watch most carefully for him Mar-shall. You can count on Jalal."

Ethan came back on.

"Well, my computer time is up. I'll email you and let you know when I can Skype again. Have fun at graduation. If things go well here I should be back before Christmas."

"Okay, be careful," Marshall said. "Oh and Ethan, I love you."

"I love you too buddy."

Ethan shut down the window.

"Why does he say he loves you?" Jalal said.

"He says he loves me as I love him. We are like brothers. It's not the kind of love like between a man and woman."

Jalal nodded. "Oh, I see. Is it wrong for Jalal to say he loves Eee-thon and Ru-sell?"

Ethan put his arm around the boy and hugged him.

"It's just fine to say that, and me to say I love you too Jalal."

The kid smiled and his eyes filled with tears.

"Jalal has no one who loves him from his people. All of my family are gone and most of my friends are afraid to be with me because I am with the soldiers."

"Why would they be afraid?"

"They are afraid if the bad men from the Taliban see them with me and they know I am with the soldiers, they may kidnap my friends and hurt them."

"Are you in danger?"

"Jalal is very careful."

"Well, don't do anything to get yourself into trouble on our account," Ethan said.

"I will be very careful. My friends watch the bad men and tell me what they are doing. I will let you know if I hear something that will help you. I want the USA to kill all of the Taliban and make our country safe."

Ethan felt sorry for the kid. There had been a war going on for decades in Afghanistan. Kids like Jalal had never known anything but war. He truly hoped that what they were doing would end up with a kid like Jalal having some kind of a future that didn't include war and killing.

"Well, its time for chow," Ethan said.

Jalal grinned from ear to ear.

"That is like music to my ears," he said.

54

Ethan's commanding officer called him and Stewart to his quarters and told them of an upcoming village celebration.

"The elders are concerned that there may be trouble so I want you to take the dogs and a squad of guys and just mill around in the crowd to make sure things go well. We've made a lot of progress with these folks and we'd like to let them see that we're on their side."

Ethan and the squad made everything ready and were leaving when Jalal came running up.

"Eee-than, I must speak to you before you go," he said excitedly.

"What's wrong?" Ethan asked.

"I have talked to my friend who lives in the village and he says that there is a rumor that someone will be at the celebration wearing a bomb. He does not know who it is but he says that there is talk of it happening."

Ethan called the guys together and told them the news.

"We'll take the dogs and mill around. If we get close to anyone who is wearing explosives they'll alert. If that happens we need to get whoever it is down and out of there before he can detonate his bomb. So we all need to watch and be ready at any moment," he said.

They made plans on how to divide and try to find the bomber and set out for the village. Jalal wanted to go along but Ethan made him stay behind.

"It's too dangerous for you Jalal," Ethan said.

"We're all wearing armor, and we have guns. You aren't protected. What happens if the bad guys grab you and kidnap you?"

"Jalal is very quick," he said.

"You stay here," Ethan said. "We'll be back in less than an hour."

The entire squad was very tense and ready for action. Ethan and Toby Stewart separated and led the dogs through the crowds of people who were celebrating some local holiday. They were eating kabobs and drinking strong coffee and all seemed very merry and happy.

Russell walked with his head up testing the air. A bunch of kids came running up and asked if they could pet him. Ethan let them and the dog acted friendly but he was still on alert.

The kids ran off and they continued through the village. Ethan could see on the next street and saw Stewart and Thor and the rest of the squad doing the same thing. They were coming to a large group of people when he noticed Jalal waving to him from behind a hut.

He was pointing to a woman carrying a pail.

"Eee-than," he pointed to the woman. "*Khathar!*" "Danger!"

Suddenly Russell's nose began going full speed. He looked at the woman and sat down.

"Dog alert!" Ethan shouted.

The "woman" turned and Ethan could see the top of a beard underneath the veil. It was a man.

"The woman! It's a man!" Ethan yelled.

Russell took off on a dead run at the guy posing as a woman and jumped from five feet away. Just at the same time a rock came from somewhere and hit the guy in the side of the head knocking him to the ground. The terrorist was fumbling trying to get his hand into his robes and Russell clamped down on his wrist and began shaking him and growling. Within a few seconds several of the other soldiers were there and had the guy sprawled on his face, handcuffing him.

The squad trained their guns on him. Ethan pulled his robes open and he was wearing a suicide vest. The detonator was within a few inches of his hand.

Ethan looked around confused. Then he saw Jalal with a big grin on his face.

"Jalal, did you throw that rock?"

"Jalal is good thrower yes? Americans teached Jalal to be baseball player. Jalal threw a beanball."

Ethan laughed and shook his head. "I thought I told you to stay in camp."

"Eee-than, Jalal promised Mar-shall to take care of you. Jalal must keep his promise."

The village elders were very excited about the apprehension of the bomber and praised Ethan and the soldiers. Jalal was grinning from ear to ear as Ethan told them how he'd beaned the guy with a rock.

When they got back to camp everyone was in good spirits.

"We did a good job today," Ethan's commander said.

"Yes sir, and thanks to Jalal, no one was hurt."

"You have quite a team, two amazing dogs and a superman kid."

There was a special treat for them that night at the mess tent. Jalal and the dogs each got a big bowl of ice cream.

"Jalal likes this wonderful cold thing," he said. "America is a wonderful place to make things such as this."

"Yes, America is a wonderful place," Ethan said. Inside he felt sad though. He knew in a few more weeks he'd be heading home and Jalal would still be in this desolate place with a very grim future.

55

The next weeks passed without incident. Thor and Russell found bombs on several trips out. Jalal came into the hut one day wearing a pair of shorts and a Nike tee shirt. He also had a baseball cap on his head. Just like many American kids, he was wearing it backwards. He was very proud of his new American clothes.

"Eee-than, Jalal is now like a real American," he said showing off his new clothes.

"Where did you get those?" Ethan asked.

"One of the men had his family send me a Caring Package," he said.

Ethan laughed. "We call it a Care Package, you look very handsome in the new outfit.

Jalal was all smiles. "Just like the American boys," he said.

Ethan smiled but inside he knew that Jalal would never know the freedom and wonderful things that American boys have. It made him very sad.

Ethan was one week away from leaving for home. Their replacements were due in a few days and they'd all be together for a couple of days to fill them in. Then they were on the planes home.

Ethan didn't say anything to Jalal, simply because he didn't know what to tell him.

They had orders to clear a road that led up to a mountain village. Some important elders were going to travel up there and the brass wanted them to get there in one piece.

The squad spread out like usual with Ethan and Stewart on point, one on each side of the road with the dogs sniffing. They were ¾ of a mile out of the village when Ethan heard shouting.

"Eee-than, they are waiting, they are waiting."

He turned and saw Jalal on the side of the hill pointing up toward a goat shed. Then a shot rang out and the rocks about ten feet in front of him burst in a cloud of dust.

"What a poor shot," he thought to himself. "If that's one of their snipers, he's about the worst sniper in the whole country."

"Eee-than, a bomb is near, run!"

He looked again and saw Jalal running down the hill with a man in a black turban chasing him. The squad went on alert and took aim at the man in the turban but Jalal was too close to be safe so they held fire.

Then from above them on the hill rifle fire began raining down on them.

"Snipers!" someone shouted.

Ethan started toward Jalal just as the Taliban guy grabbed him and started dragging him up the hill. Jalal jerked his arm free and got away and ran toward Ethan.

Another slug hit the dirt in front of him and then he noticed Russell was alerting.

"Bomb, take cover," he shouted. "Russell, out, out, out!"

Now he knew what was happening. The sniper was shooting at the bomb trying to set it off with a slug.

"Eee-than, run!" Jalal screamed.

Russell saw the man chasing Jalal and broke away from Ethan and ran up the hill toward him. When he was five feet away he leapt off the rocks and hit the man mid-chest, knocking him down. Then he grabbed him by the throat and began shaking him. The guy screamed and grabbed at Russell and hit him with his fist. The dog yelped and landed on his side on the ground. The Taliban sat up and was reaching for a knife on his belt and Jalal smashed him in the head with a rock. He fell backward, stunned and Russell and Jalal ran toward Ethan.

The guy got to a sitting position and someone shot him and he went down in a cloud of dust. Russell and Jalal were running toward Ethan. He turned to run back away from the bomb.

"Oh God! Toby, get Thor out. They're trying to detonate with a bullet! Go back!" he shouted to the rest of the squad. "Get away they're shooting at the bomb."

Jalal realized he was going the wrong way. He was running toward the bomb. He turned and called Russell to follow him. Ethan heard another shot from the goat shed. He looked and Toby and Thor were much too close to the bomb.

"Toby get away! They're trying to set it off with a bullet!"

Stewart shouted to Thor and they turned to run.

Then it was like the world went to slow motion. The closest squad members had turned and were running from the bomb. Toby and Thor had their backs to it and were going as fast as they could from it. Jalal and Russell were climbing up the hill as fast as they could. Ethan had taken four steps when it went off.

There was a deafening explosion. All Ethan could feel was heat and immense pressure as the bomb detonated. Ethan knew what had happened. He could hear nothing. His eyes failed and all he saw was blackness but he knew he was falling and his last conscious thought was that he would never see his parents or Marshall again.

56

Marshall woke and lay with his arm around Buzzie. The dog was snuggled up next to him and was snoring loudly. Marshall smiled at the little dog and was glad to have him with him. It had been lonely the past months without Ethan.

He looked at the alarm clock and he figured he had nearly an hour left to sleep or nap in bed. He'd started working at the family hardware store after graduation and surprisingly didn't mind the job. There was always something to do and always customers to help, so the time passed quickly.

He was just about to drift off to sleep when he heard talking downstairs. He opened his eyes and listened. At first he thought it was his parents but then he heard more voices. After listening for a minute he figured it out that it was Ethan's parents voices. What were they doing at his house so early in the morning?

Suddenly he felt a cold chill run down his spine. Something must have happened to Ethan. That was the only reason they'd be downstairs so early.

Marshall jumped out of bed and pulled on his shorts. He didn't bother with a shirt or shoes and hurried down the stairs. He walked quickly into the kitchen, his hair wild and stopped short.

His mom was holding Ethan's mom and she was crying. The two dads turned and looked at him and he could see on their faces that something was terribly wrong.

"Dad?" he said looking at his father.

"Marshall, there's something we need to tell you," his dad said.

"Oh no!" Marshall said. He felt his knees wobbling and grabbed the countertop. His dad stepped up and helped him to a chair.

Marshall's eyes were full of tears.

"Marshall, he's not dead, he's been hurt... very badly," Ethan's dad said.

"He's not dead? Oh God, thank you God," Marshall said.

"A roadside bomb went off and he was close to it. We don't know for sure all of the details but Ethan was hurt and the other bomb dog and his handler were killed. He's in Germany at the hospital at our base there."

"What's hurt on him?"

"He's had a massive trauma to both his legs and his left arm. He took a hard blow to the head and there is a lot of shrapnel. Right now it's touch and go."

Marshall felt his insides turn to jelly. It didn't seem possible. Ethan was always so perfect, so handsome and so strong and now he was hurt so badly that he might not live or might be crippled. It just was hard to comprehend.

"Are we going to Germany?" he said.

"No Marshall, they're going to bring him to Washington as soon as they get him stabilized. He'll be at Walter Reed Hospital... unless."

"Don't say unless. He'll be okay and I'll be with him until he is," Marshall said.

"Okay, no unless," Ethan's dad said.

"So what do we do in the meantime?" Marshall said.

"What do you mean?"

"I mean who do we talk to and where will we stay when we go to Washington to be with Ethan?"

"I uh, I'm not sure Marshall, but I'll find out."

Marshall turned to his dad.

"You'll have to get along without me until Ethan is better and can come home," he said.

His dad smiled.

"So you're planning on going to Washington and staying there until he's better?"

"Of course. I'm going upstairs and get on the computer. I'll find out what needs to be done and as soon as he's in the hospital there, I'm going."

And he marched off upstairs.

"I have a phone number where I can update his status. As soon as I hear one way or the other I'll let you know," Ethan's dad said.

"I'll call in someone to take your place at the store. I guess I better get someone for Marshall too, he's probably packing right now."

"I hope to God he will need to pack," Ethan's mom said.

57

The call came the next morning from the hospital in Germany. Ethan had been stabilized and was being treated for his wounds. He was unconscious and that was something that wasn't a worry yet.

The military had him scheduled to be on a flight from Germany and he would arrive the next day in Washington. Ethan's dad came to the house and went to Marshall's room.

"I got a call from Germany. He's stable and they're going to fly him to Washington tomorrow. They didn't tell me what's wrong with him but he's still unconscious. They don't seem concerned about that because they'd have kept him sedated anyway.

"So when are we leaving?" Marshall asked.

"Marshall are you sure you want to go? We don't know how bad he is, it might be traumatic."

"Ethan has been there for me my whole life. Every time I got a scrape, or banged my knee, he was there. He saved my life in Canada when we crashed the plane. I have to be there for him. Don't you see? I've got some money for a plane ticket. If I have to I'll beg on the street to get money to eat and sleep when I get there. I want to be there for him and I want to stay with him until he's ready to come home."

Ethan's dad hugged the kid.

"Ethan is a lucky guy to have a friend like you," he said quietly.

"So I can go?"

"We've already got the tickets. You and I and his mom are going. We have a place to stay when we get there and once we see how long he'll be in the hospital we'll figure the rest out."

Marshall smiled and nodded.

"He'll be okay. He's the toughest guy I've ever known. I just know he'll be okay."

Marshall's parents took them to the airport the next day and saw them off. Marshall had packed as much as he could get into a large duffel bag. They landed in DC and took a taxi to the hospital.

When they checked at the front desk they were given Ethan's room number and they left their luggage in a secure area until they could return.

As they went up in the elevator Marshall's knees were knocking. He didn't know what to expect and he wasn't sure he was ready for it. They got to the correct floor and walked down several hallways until they found the room.

"Are you okay?" Ethan's dad said to his mom.

"I'm shaking but I'm ready to see him," she said. She took Marshall's hand. "Let's go," she said.

Marshall pushed the door open. There was a curtain around the bed and the room was dimly lit. They could hear several machines beeping and clicking and they walked toward the curtain.

"Are you family?" a voice came from a little room off to the side.

They turned and a nurse stepped out of the room. She was a large black lady wearing what looked like a pajama top and turquoise pants.

"We're his parents and this is his best friend."

"He's stable. I want to warn you he looks pretty tough. He took a massive blow from the explosion but the doctors in Germany managed to save both of his legs. His arm has been set and he is pretty well covered with bandages. I just checked his vital signs and they look good. His blood pressure is very good and everything seems to be working. It's a lot better when the injured is a strong young man like he is. He's still sleeping but that's common. He took a good jolt to the head and there's some swelling in his brain. That's coming along okay too. So, you go ahead and see him. He probably can't hear you but if you want to talk to him, do it anyway."

They looked at each other. Marshall was nearly afraid to open the curtain.

Ethan's dad pulled the curtain back and his mom gasped.

Marshall felt like he was going to pass out. His ears began to ring and he felt unsteady. He took hold of the rail of the bed and steadied himself.

The person in the bed could have been anyone. Both of his legs were wrapped from the hip to his feet in bandages. There were drains coming out of the wraps. His left arm was also bandaged and in a plastic cast. Most of his head was wrapped in bandages. The only part of him showing was his right eye and his mouth. There was a breathing tube taped to his cheek and it went down his throat.

His mom began to cry as she took hold of his right hand. His dad looked very pale and his hands were shaking.

Marshall's eyes filled with tears and he touched Ethan's shoulder.

"God Almighty,' he said.

58

The next few days were a mix of hours of sitting by Ethan's bed, talking to doctors and riding in taxis back and forth from the hospital to the motel. Marshall was getting to know the nurses and orderlies and doctors as he spent nearly every minute at the side of his best friend's bed.

Ethan slept. Now and then he'd stir but otherwise he was still and oblivious to what was going on. Marshall talked to him sitting next the bed on a chair. He talked about fishing and baseball and anything else that he could think of to talk about. Each day the nurses and doctors came in and changed the bandages on his legs. The first time Marshall nearly fainted when he saw the injuries to the lower part of Ethan's legs.

When the bomb exploded Ethan was running away and slightly downhill. His feet were mostly protected in his boots and were down low where the shrapnel from the bomb missed them. His calves were hurt the worst. Both legs had been broken and the muscles were torn and ripped apart. The doctors felt that they could save his legs and did the best they could. They'd performed hours of surgery to repair all of the damage. Now the threat was from infection. If the legs became infected Ethan still might lose them.

Each day the doctor looked and was pleased that there were no signs of infection. Every day the legs looked better. The stitches were removed and one by one the drains were also removed. The damage healed and the angry red color faded. Each day Marshall said a prayer of thanks.

At the end of the week Ethan's parents talked to Marshall about what to do next. Ethan would be in the hospital for months. They felt it was necessary for one of them to stay with him but Marshall shook his head.

"I'll stay with him," Marshall said

"Oh honey, we can't ask you to do that," Ethan's mom said.

"I'm going to stay either way. If you guys stay, I'm staying. If you go home, I'm still staying. I'm going to be here until he's ready to go home."

Ethan's mom hugged Marshall.

"You love him like a brother don't you?" she said.

"He's the only brother I've ever known," Marshall said. "You guys need to get back and work. The store can operate without me. I just can't leave," he said.

"But this is a lot to put onto a boy your age," Ethan's dad said.

"Ethan would do it for me. I know he would. I want to be here when he wakes up and I want to be here when he walks out of this hospital. One way or the other I am going to be here."

They talked to a lady who helped with family placement and she found a local man who offered a room to anyone who needed one so they could be with wounded soldiers. Ethan's dad gave Marshall a credit card for food and anything else he needed.

"You call us if there's any change," his mom said. "Promise us."

"I'll call every day. He's going to be okay, I'll bring him home," he said.

They hugged the boy and left for home.

Marshall sat in his chair by the bed and took hold of Ethan's one good hand.

"I'm here yet," he said. "Your mom and dad went back to Wisconsin. I'm in charge now. As soon as you wake up, I'll be here. Okay?"

Marshall wasn't sure but he thought he felt Ethan squeeze his hand slightly.

He smiled and squeezed back.

He took a bus to the address he'd been given and knocked on the front door of a big two-story house in a quiet neighborhood about half an hour from the hospital. A man who looked to be in his sixties or seventies greeted him and ask him to come in.

"You must be Marshall," the man said.

"Yes sir," he said.

"I'm Harry," the man said.

"I want to thank you for offering me a room Harry," Marshall said.

"I'm happy to help. I live alone in this big old house and it's good to have someone to talk to now and then. How is your friend doing?"

"So far it's going okay," Marshall said. He explained Ethan's injuries and how the threat of infection was still there.

"They'll fix him up, they know what they're doing there," Harry said.

He showed Marshall his room and where the bathroom and kitchen was. Then he made them something to eat. Marshall liked the old man. He felt at home in this strange house and knew everything was going to be all right... eventually.

The next day he was telling Ethan about Harry and his room. He talked as he usually did and had no idea if he could hear him or not. He looked down at the foot of the bed and saw the toes on Ethan's left foot moving.

"Hey," he said, "You're wiggling your toes."

He looked at Ethan and gasped. His right eye was open and he was looking at him.

"Holy crap, you're awake," Marshall said.

Ethan gripped Marshall's hand and blinked.

"Just wait there, I gotta go get the nurse," Marshall said. He bolted from the room and then he grinned. "Just wait there? Like he's going some place?"

When he and the nurse returned Ethan was looking around the room. The nurse took his vitals and said everything was good. She called the doctor and he came into the room a short time later.

"Hello," he said. "It's good to see you awake."

Ethan blinked.

"We're going to turn down the oxygen to your breathing tube. If it is difficult to breathe close your eye. If not, just look at us, understand?"

Ethan blinked.

The doctor turned the oxygen flow down a little and Ethan seemed okay. They waited a minute and shut down the flow a little more and Ethan seemed okay.

"Okay I'm going to turn if off."

Ethan looked at the doctor and then at Marshall.

"Let's get that tube out of your throat," the doctor said.

They pulled the tape off and told Ethan to take a deep breath and then blow it out. When he did they pulled the tube up from his throat. He gagged and his eye watered but he seemed to be okay.

"Better?"

Ethan nodded.

"I know you'll feel better now," Marshall said. "I remember when they did that to me and it was so much better without that tube in my throat."

Ethan nodded.

Marshall was smiling as wide as possible.

59

O ver the next weeks things got much better. The bandages on Ethan's face were removed. The last of the drains in his legs were removed and the bandages got smaller and smaller. His wounds healed and he got stronger each day.

Ethan's voice was very scratchy. The tube in his throat had made his vocal cords rough and he talked like he was very hoarse.

Marshall kept the families apprised of his recovery and they were very happy to hear the news each day. Each day they thought they should return and each time Marshall told them he had everything taken care of.

Though Ethan was recovering physically, he seemed very quiet and very sad.

Ethan didn't have a heavy beard but he'd grown some facial hair and the nurse asked him if he'd like a shave. He said yes and she gave Marshall the job.

He was there from morning to night every day and kind of became a part of the staff unofficially. They raised Ethan's bed so he was sitting part way up and Marshall lathered up his face and began shaving him.

"You're probably in more danger right now than you were over there," he joked as he dragged the razor across Ethan's throat.

Ethan gave him a weak smile.

Marshall finished up the shave and wiped his face off with a warm cloth.

"There, you look pretty darn good," he said.

"Thanks," Ethan said.

Marshall knew that Ethan was hurting inside and didn't know for sure what to do about it.

"Ethan what can I do to cheer you up?"

"Nobody will tell me about what happened. I need to know."

"No one has told you?"

Ethan shook his head.

"I don't know if I'm suppose to tell you, but what I've been told was that the bad guys shot at a roadside bomb and set it off."

"I know that. What happened to the rest?"

"You mean the other guys?"

He nodded.

"Ethan your buddy Toby Stewart and his dog were killed. Three others died also. There was an ambush. One of them died from the bomb and two were shot by snipers."

Ethan's eyes filled with tears.

"Russell?"

Marshall thought back to what he'd been told.

"I don't know. No one has ever said a word about him."

"What about Jalal?"

"Cripes, I don't know. I didn't even think about him. Holy crap, I don't know Ethan."

Ethan nodded and closed his eyes.

"It was my fault," he said.

"How was it your fault, the bad guys attacked you and set off the bomb, that wasn't your fault."

"I should have warned them. I missed it. I didn't see Russell alert. I should have warned them sooner. I got them all killed."

"Ethan you had no way of knowing they'd shoot at a bomb. And we don't know for sure if the dog and the kid were killed."

"I need to know."

"Ethan, I'll find out. I'll be back."

Marshall walked down the hall and took an elevator up to the top floor. This was where the big important people were. He went into the office of the hospital director and asked to talk to the top guy.

He was asked what it was about and he told the secretary. She went into an office and soon came back.

"He can spare a few minutes."

Marshall walked in and there sat an officer with a chest full of ribbons. He told him what he was trying to find out.

"We don't have that information but I can make some inquiries," the man said.

He said he'd send the information to the nurse on Ethan's floor as soon as he got it. That seemed good enough for Marshall, so he returned and gave Ethan the message.

"It's all my fault," Ethan said.

"No way Ethan. You didn't do anything wrong."

"I took my eye off the job. Jalal was there and some of the bad guys were carrying him off. Russell saw that and went to aid him. I should have pulled him out and let everyone know what was happening. I messed up. I was worrying about Jalal and got my guys killed."

"Ethan they were shooting at you and the bomb. There was nothing you could do."

"I got my guys killed and probably got Russell and Jalal killed too."

He turned his head away from him and Marshall could see he was crying. He'd never seen this big strong guy shed a tear in all the years they'd been friends and it broke his heart to see him crying now. He took hold of Ethan's hand and held it. He didn't know what else to do.

60

Marshall was sitting in Harry's kitchen picking at a plate of eggs and bacon. Harry sat across from him watching.

"What's troubling you Marshall? I've never seen a kid your age that let a plate of food sit in front of them like that."

"I'm worried about Ethan," Marshall said. "He's so depressed. He thinks it's his fault that some of his friends got killed. We can't seem to find out what happened to his dog and to the kid who was with them."

"He's got survivor's guilt," Harry said.

"What's that?"

"It happens when someone dies and someone lives. The person that lives feels guilty that they made it and their friends didn't. It can be a hard thing to get over. You say he can't find out about his dog? This was a military dog... right?"

"Yeah, he was a bomb dog. No one seems to know what happened to him. Ethan just can't seem to get over it."

"Maybe I can help."

"How can you do that Harry?"

"I'm retired from the Marines. I was a Colonel and I know a lot of people in the right places. Let me make some phone calls today and I'll see what I can find out."

"Oh Harry, that'd be good. I talked to a big shot at the hospital but I don't think he was really too interested in finding anything out. Of course he has so many people to take care of."

"Well don't tell Ethan. I'll see what I can find out first."

Marshall was feeling better as he got off the bus and walked into the hospital. He'd just talked to his parents and called Ethan's parents and given them the news that Ethan was now off all of the machines and catheters and was going to start physical therapy today. Ethan was in a wheelchair when he walked into the room.

"Hey, are you going for a ride?" he asked.

"Physical therapy," Ethan said.

"Cool, is it okay if I come and watch?"

"Suit yourself," Ethan replied.

A nurse came in and Marshall walked with them to the therapy room. There were soldiers all over the room working with therapists. Some were missing legs, some were missing arms and some were missing both.

A large black man in shorts and a tight white tee shirt came over and introduced himself.

"I'm Franklin Pierce," he said. "You can call me Frank."

"Ethan Randall," Ethan said.

"And this is?" he said looking at Marshall.

"I'm Marshall, I'm his best friend."

Frank smiled. "I've heard you're here every day."

Marshall nodded. "I'll be here until he's ready to go home."

Frank grinned. "Well then let's go to work and get him ready."

Frank put Ethan through a series of exercises that made him work to get his legs and arms back to the strength they once had. Ethan gritted his teeth and winced in pain many times but didn't complain. Marshall did what he could do to help and his heart hurt to see Ethan working so hard but looking so glum.

After an hour Ethan was bathed in sweat and Frank said he'd had enough.

"You did great for your first time," he said.

"Tomorrow will be easier and it'll get easier every day after that."

Marshall wheeled Ethan back to his room. He asked the nurse about cleaning him up.

"Why don't you take him to the showers? I know you and he are very good friends. If he doesn't mind and you don't mind, take some clean clothes and help him take a shower. You can wheel him right in and then he can sit on a plastic chair. If you need help, just pull the cord and someone will be there to help you."

"Cool, I can do that," Marshall said, glad to be doing something useful.

He told Ethan what they were going to do and he said it was fine with him. Marshall got a clean pair of boxers and shorts and a tee shirt and wheeled him to the showers. There were three other patients in the big shower room being assisted by orderlies. Marshall saw how they were doing it and helped Ethan get out of his sweaty clothes. Then he wheeled him next to a plastic chair with arm rests and took him by his bad arm while Ethan gripped one handle with his good arm. Together they got him onto the chair and Marshall turned on the shower.

Ethan yelped when the water hit him.

"Shit! It's like ice!" he shouted.

"Oops, sorry," Marshall said turning the hot water on. Soon the temperature was adjusted. Marshall took off his shoes and socks and helped Ethan wash his legs and back while Ethan washed his body.

Marshall squirted some shampoo on Ethan's head and washed his hair for him.

"Your hair is growing out again," he said. "It's getting a little curly too."

He pushed him under the water and rinsed him off. Then he shut the water off and together they got him dried off. Marshall helped him get is boxers and shorts on and then Ethan slid the tee shirt over his head.

"Well, that was quite a production," Marshall said.

"Thanks," Ethan replied.

"Anything I can do, you know I will," Marshall said.

Ethan looked at him. "I know."

61

Marshall wheeled Ethan back to his room and helped him into bed. Ethan was obviously very tired so he shut off the light and let him sleep for a while.

He was a bit hungry so he took the elevator down to the cafeteria and got a piece of pie and a glass of milk. He looked out over the many tables and saw Franklin Pierce sitting alone so he walked over to his table.

"Hey Marshall, have a seat," Pierce said smiling.

"Done for the day?" Marshall asked.

"No I'm just taking a break. Ethan is coming along well."

"Yeah, he's getting stronger all the time. Thanks to you."

"I'm just doing my job Marshall."

"You act like you really enjoy your work," Marshall said.

"It's the best job in the world. I get a chance to take someone who is broken and has given up and make him back into a full person who has a life ahead of him."

"What kind of school do you need for it?"

Franklin grinned.

"You thinking of doing something like this?"

"I'm really impressed with how you guys get these soldiers to do stuff that no one would expect them to do. It's really amazing. I had no idea what I wanted to do with my life, but I think I'd enjoy a job like this."

"There are PT jobs for a lot of other things too. When people have surgery they need PT to get back in shape. Older people need it to keep moving. It pays well too. There is a fair amount of science involved in the schooling but a bright guy like you would sail through it."

"You think I could do it?"

Franklin smiled.

"I think you'd be a great therapist. I've seen how you help Ethan and some of the others. Your heart is in it Marshall. You'd do well."

"Hmm, I'm going to think about that. It'd beat the heck out of selling nuts and bolts for the rest of my life."

Franklin laughed and pushed his chair back.

"See you later Marshall. Think about that idea. The world needs guys like you to make others whole again."

Marshall watched the massive man walk off. Dang, he might just have found something to do with his life after all.

He ate his pie and went back up to Ethan's room. Ethan was still sleeping. There was a comfortable chair in the corner by the bed and Marshall sat back in it and soon was sleeping too. He woke when he smelled food.

An orderly had brought Ethan's lunch into the room. Ethan was awake but wasn't eating.

"What's for lunch?" Marshall said.

Ethan shrugged. "Not very hungry," he said.

"Ethan you have to eat. You're skinny already. How do you expect to get well if you don't eat?"

Ethan didn't answer. He just turned his head away.

"Ethan I'm going to find Russell."

He turned back toward Marshall.

"He's alive?"

"I've got somebody who has connections looking into it. If Russell is alive I'll find him. I promise."

"But you don't know?"

"Not yet. But I will. Ethan you know me. If I get something in my head I'm going to hang onto it like a bulldog until I get it done."

Ethan smiled for the first time in a long time.

"You got that right. You're the most stubborn shit I've ever known."

Marshall nodded. "Okay, so eat your lunch."

Ethan picked up his fork.

"Okay boss."

Harry reported making some calls that evening; friends in the Pentagon were looking into the missing dog. He couldn't promise anything but he had good people looking.

The next day Ethan and Marshall went to physical therapy again and Ethan worked hard. Frank added a few repetitions of each exercise and was merciless on him.

"Hard work will make you whole again," he said.

After a shower and lunch Marshall got a call. It was from Harry. Ethan was napping so he stepped out into the hall.

"Hey, I just wanted to let you know. I've found a chopper pilot who was there when Ethan's squad got ambushed. He flew some of the injured out of there. He said one dog was dead but he saw another dog and a kid running up the mountain away from the battle.

"Was it a golden retriever?"

"He said it was a yellow dog."

"Oh man, that's probably Russell and Jalal. The kid was kind of like a homeless kid they'd taken in."

"Okay, well at least we know they made it through the battle. Now I have to find someone to find them somewhere, in Afghanistan."

"Can you do that Harry?"

"If they're still alive, I'll find them."

"What should I tell Ethan?"

"Don't get his hopes up. You better wait until we have more information."

Marshall was very excited. Russell might be okay. If that was the case it would make Ethan's recovery much faster. He hoped and prayed it was possible that the dog and the kid were still out there someplace.

Ethan was sleeping so Marshall went down the hall to a room with computers that the soldiers could use. If Russell was alive, he needed help to get him back to the states and to get him to the hospital. He needed a US Senator.

62

Marshall felt underdressed. The only clothes he had with him in Washington in addition to boxers were shorts and tee shirts, a pair of sneakers and a pair of flip-flops.

He approached the door to the Senate Office Building and asked for directions to the office of Senator Ron Johnson of Wisconsin. He followed the directions and found the office. Inside a middle-aged lady welcomed him and offered him a seat while she let the Senator know he had a visitor. Soon she came back and showed him to an inner office.

Senator Johnson was sitting behind his desk wearing a light blue shirt with the sleeves rolled up and was without a tie. He got up and shook hands with Marshall and told him to have a seat.

"So I understand you have a friend who's been injured and there is a bomb dog missing?"

Marshall nodded and told him the whole story of Ethan and them being friends for life and how Ethan blamed himself for what happened in Afghanistan. Senator Johnson listened and nodded now and then.

"I think if we could find Russell and bring him back here, Ethan would come out of his funk and he'd be better in no time. I've known him for all of my life and I've never seen him like this. It's like he doesn't want to get better."

Senator Johnson picked up the phone and made a call and relayed the story to someone on the other end. He listened a bit and then said to keep him advised.

"I've got an aide working on it. He'll get Ethan's records from Walter Reed and track down his squad. I understand you have an ex-military man working on it too. Give him my personal number and have him give me anything he finds out. We'll do what we can and if we can find... Russell is it? We'll bring him home."

Marshall was all smiles. He thanked the Senator and left feeling better than he had in a long time. When he got back to the hospital he had a hard time not to tell Ethan what was going on. He didn't want to get his hopes up and if Russell was really dead, it would be worse for Ethan if he had hope and then it turned out badly.

The next few days were pretty much routine. He went to the hospital, went with Ethan to physical therapy, helped him shower and then kept him company for the rest of the day. Ethan was gaining strength every day and looking more like the old Ethan but his spirit was still broken. His hair had grown out and covered the red scars on his head and his wounds looked better each day.

He had been very pale but now he had some color in his cheeks again and physically, he looked like he was ready to go home. His mental health was still in question.

Three nights later when Marshall took the bus to Harry's house Harry was waiting on the front porch. He was smiling so Marshall was curious.

"Have you found anything?" he asked.

"That I have," Harry said. "I talked to the Senator today and they're sending a squad to the place where Ethan was hurt. The local elders have confided in one of our officers that there is a boy and a dog living in the mountains and they are helping them. They dare not come into the village because the Taliban is looking for the boy. They know he has helped the Americans and if they found him it would not be a good thing."

"Oh man, so Jalal is alive too," Marshall said.

"It would seem so," Harry replied.

"So what happens next?"

"Our guys will see if they can find the boy and the dog and if they do, they'll put them on a plane."

"Oh my gosh, they'll bring them here?"

"That's what he said. United States Senators have a lot of clout. I think Senator Johnson is one of the good ones. When he says something, he does it. If all goes right they should be here in a few days, a week at the most."

Marshall jumped up from the chair and hugged Harry.

"Harry you're the best," he said.

The old man blinked hard. "Thanks Marshall, it's been a long time since I had a kid who thought I was anything but an old fossil."

"You are THE MAN!" Marshall said.

"How about some ice cream?" Harry said.

"I'll scoop," Marshall said as they walked into the house.

63

The nights were getting colder and colder. In a few weeks winter would set in and the weather would be very cold and there would be much snow. Jalal and Russell were huddled in a small cave half way up the mountain above the village. They'd made the place livable by stealing some straw from the goat shed down the hill a little way and by covering the opening with an old tarp that they'd stolen from a house down in the valley. Russell was lying with his head on Jalal's lap.

"Ru-sell, we must find a new place soon to be living," he said to the dog. "The bad men will find us if we stay here many more time."

Russell looked up and nuzzled the boy. Jalal smiled at him.

"Ru-sell, how would I have gotten so far without you? If you had not attacked that bad man I would be dead now."

He hugged the dog. "We would both be dead... like Eee-than."

His eyes filled with tears.

"Eee-than, and Stew-wart and Thor are all gone. My good friends all gone," he said sadly.

Just then Russell's ears perked up. He looked into the shadows and growled quietly.

Jalal was on alert. He looked carefully for movement and then saw something move near the trail below them. He smiled widely as his friend Omar appeared carrying a basket.

"Jalal, hello, how are you?" he said.

"Omar, Jalal is glad to see you. What have you brought us?"

Omar was one of Jalal's friends who snuck up to his hiding place and brought them food and water and whatever else they could steal or beg.

"I have bread and some cheese and some goat meat. I also

have another blanket for you."

Jalal and Russell were very glad to see their friend. They spread the food out and Jalal shared it with Russell. Omar told them of the things going on in the village.

"The Taliban are looking for you Jalal. You must be very careful if you leave this cave. They will do very bad things to you if they find you."

"I know this. Omar we must find a new place soon. It will start to get cold and this place will not be good for us when the winter comes."

"We will look for a new place," Omar said. "I will ask the elders."

"Be very careful," Jalal said.

"Always," Omar replied. "I must return to the village. Be safe Jalal."

They hugged and Omar disappeared into the darkness.

"Ru-sell, tonight we have full bellies. This is good. But tomorrow, we will have to see how God treats us."

He pulled the new blanket over the dog and himself and they nestled down and soon were sleeping.

Below, in the village, several American vehicles were just pulling into the old compound where the Americans had lived before the ambush.

64

The sky was just beginning brighten. Jalal was wrapped in his blanket with Russell. It had been a cold night but the dog was very warm and it was like sleeping with another person.

Suddenly Russell raised his head and a low growl came from deep inside his chest.

Jalal woke instantly.

"Ru-sell, what is it?" he said. He stared into the darkness. It was just light enough to begin to make out single boulders and rocks from the blackness. He watched down the hillside looking carefully for movement.

"Is it the bad men?" he whispered.

The dog whined.

Jalal heard a voice. He couldn't make out what it said but it sounded like it was someone speaking English.

"Ru-sell, is it soldiers?"

The dog whined again and wagged his tail.

Jalal watched and soon he saw movement. The figure was dressed in dark clothes and was carrying a rifle. Then he saw a second figure.

His heart was beating hard. Should he run or should he hope they didn't find him in his little hole in the ground?

Then he heard a young voice. It was Omar. He saw his friend scampering up the hill toward his hiding place.

"See... here, he is here!" Omar said excitedly.

Jalal looked up at his friend and then behind him. There were two American soldiers standing there and several more down the hill farther.

"Are you Jalal?" one of them asked.

"I am Jalal, and who are you?"

The soldier laughed. "They told us you were pretty cocky. We're here to rescue you. We're here because someone very important in the USA wants you to be safe."

"Jalal is a very important translator and finder of good things," the kid said grinning.

"Yeah I bet so, is the dog in there with you?"

"Ru-sell and I are here together," he replied.

The soldier turned to the others. "It's him," he said.

"We're here to take you with us. Gather up your stuff."

"I have nothing but a blanket and what I am wearing."

"Well, leave the blanket and let's go."

Jalal crawled out of the hole and Russell came out wagging his tail. He went right up to the soldiers. He was happy to see them and looked at each one carefully as if he was looking for one in particular.

"He's looking for Eee-than," Jalal said. "But Eee-than is dead and I cannot explain that to a dog."

"Sergeant Randall isn't dead," the soldier said.

Jalal looked astonished. "We saw him when the bomb exploded. He was too close."

"He was injured badly but he's alive. I'm not sure of the exact story but he seems to have a friend from home that has been with him for weeks. The kid has worked some kind of magic and has the Pentagon and a US Senator helping him find you. We're taking you and the dog to the United States."

Jalal stood there speechless. "How is this possible?"

"Anything is possible when someone from Congress gets involved."

Jalal nodded knowingly.

"What is Congress?"

The soldier explained it to him on the way down the mountain. When they got to the compound Jalal hugged Omar and thanked him for helping him all these weeks.

"So you will go to America?" Omar asked.

"This is what they say," he said. "I will miss you Omar."

The two boys hugged and they both wept. Omar stepped back and looked one last time at his friend and then walked off to the village.

"I am *tafil,* smelly," Jalal said as he climbed into the vehicle.

"Yes you are. We'll get you a shower and then we can get rid of those filthy clothes. We've got stuff for you to wear. The dog gets a bath too."

They rode back to the base compound and showed Jalal to the shower tent.

It ended up that both Jalal and Russell took a shower together. The dog loved water and they ended up having a great time. When Jalal dried off he found a pair of boxers, a pair of khaki shorts and a red tee shirt waiting for him. There was also a pair of Nike sneakers.

He had never had shoes so he didn't know what to think about the wonderful shoes. When he emerged from the bath hut he was carrying the boxers.

"Jalal does not know what to do with the extra trousers," he said.

The soldiers laughed. They explained the purpose of the boxers. Jalal nodded and went back inside and came back grinning.

"So now I am properly attired?"

"That you are kid. How about some grub?"

"What is grub?"

"Food."

"Okey-dokey, I have missed the American food. Jalal likes bacon cheeseburgers."

He and Russell were stuffed when they left the mess tent. It was the first time he didn't feel hungry in a long time.

65

E than was napping and Marshall was reading a magazine when his phone buzzed. He checked to see that it was Harry. He left Ethan's room so he wouldn't wake him.

"Hi Harry," he said.

"They found him," Harry said.

"Russell?"

"Russell and the kid."

"No kidding? Oh man that's great."

"Senator Johnson's office called me since you told him I was helping. They're putting him on a transport plane to Germany and then back to DC. They're not sure when he'll get here but he's on the way."

Marshall was elated. "Will Jalal be able to come too?"

"Yes, Johnson's office said they're working on a visa that will allow him to stay because he's in danger in Afghanistan. He's been helping the Americans so he'd be killed if he stayed there so he'll get refugee status. They're going to de-commission the dog and he can go home with Ethan."

"Where will Jalal go?"

"I thought I'd leave that up to you."

Marshall had a lot of calls to make.

"Harry, thanks a million, I'll get back to you. Right now I have to call our folks and I have lots to get done."

He called Ethan's parents and told them what was happening. They were very excited.

"I just know that this will get Ethan out of the hospital," Marshall said. "He thinks he's responsible for the dog and the kid's death and when he sees them he'll turn right around. I just know it."

"What will happen to the dog and the boy?"

"We have to find them a place to stay. The military will let the dog go home with Ethan. The boy needs a home."

"We'll take him," Ethan's mom said.

"Just like that?"

"Just like that... whom should I talk to?"

Marshall gave her Johnson's personal number and said he'd call back when he knew more. He went to Ethan's room and had all he could do to keep from telling him the news. He almost woke him but decided it was better to wait until they could surprise him.

Meanwhile in Afghanistan Jalal was being driven along with Russell to a military airfield near the capital. He had seen planes flying over the country but had never seen one up close. They drove up to a C130 transport and stopped.

"This is the plane that will take you to Germany," the soldier said.

Jalal looked up at the huge machine. "This machine will go up into the air?"

The soldier nodded and grinned.

"How is this possible? This machine is as big as a mountain."

"It's all physics," the soldier said.

"What is physics?"

"When you start to go to school in the USA you'll find out."

"I will go to school?"

"I expect you will. How else will you become an American?"

Jalal was all grins as he climbed up into the plane. Russell seemed at ease since part of his training was flying in aircraft and even jumping from them.

Jalal turned just before he walked into the fuselage and looked out over the rocky barren landscape that had been his home for all his life.

"*Ma' salami*" "Goodbye," he said.

66

T he next 48 hours were like a whirlwind for Jalal. There were soldiers on the first transport and they were very friendly to the boy and dog and by the time they got to Germany he felt like they were all friends. Then in Germany he experienced a modern city for the first time. He marveled at skyscrapers and the hundreds of cars and trucks. He spent the night with Russell at the military hospital sleeping on a couch since he was going to be there for such a short time. At the hospital he and Russell were a big hit too. Many of the soldiers had kids at home who they missed so a boy and a dog got a lot of attention.

The next morning he and Russell boarded another plane along with many soldiers and flew across the ocean to the United States. Jalal's mind was spinning as he looked out the windows and saw the endless miles of water below them. They flew for many hours and Jalal fell asleep with Russell in his lap. When the plane started to descend he woke and looked with awe as they landed in Washington DC. He could see many huge monuments from the air and the soldiers told him of the great men they honored. He didn't understand a lot of it but he knew he had come to a most wonderful place.

Once they landed in DC he was taken to a military base and after a meal and a shower and a change into clean clothes he was taken to his next stop... Walter Reed Hospital.

His driver parked in a huge parking lot that held hundreds of cars. Jalal marveled at the many styles and colors of them.

"Does everyone in America have such an automobile?" he asked.

"Most people do," his driver said. "American's love their cars."

"They are most wonderful," he said.

The driver took him to a huge room where many women

and men stood behind a short wall and talked to people coming into the building. He spoke to a man and the man made a phone call.

"Your friend will come and get you," he said.

"I have no friend in America," Jalal said.

"You must have someone who knows you," the driver said.

"I only have ever met one person and that was looking at him on a machine that sent images to satellites. I do not know for sure what a satellite is but I think it involves magic."

The driver laughed. "You'll learn about many magic things here kiddo."

Just then Marshall came out of an elevator and ran across the huge room toward him.

"It is Mar-shall," Jalal said, "it is Mar-shall, my friend."

Marshall ran up to them and hugged Jalal. Then he knelt down and hugged Russell. He had tears in his eyes.

"I'm so glad to see you guys," he said.

"I am very happy to see you too Mar-shall."

"Ethan is going to just crap when he sees you two."

"Eee-than is here?"

Marshall nodded.

"Eee-than is really alive?"

"Yes, he's alive and when he sees you he is going to be the happiest guy in the world.

Jalal knelt and hugged Russell. "Eee-than is here Ru-sell, Eee-than is here!"

Marshall thanked the driver. He shook hands with Marshall and then Jalal. "Good luck to you kid," he said.

Jalal gave him a thousand watt smile. "Jalal is already the luckiest boy in the world."

67

Marshall led Jalal and Russell to the bank of elevators. He pushed the UP button and a door opened on their right. They walked in and the door closed. Marshall pushed the 9th floor button.

Jalal stood looking around the elevator car.

"Why are we in this little room?" he asked.

"This is the elevator to take us to Ethan."

The kid stood looking clueless.

"This little room goes up and down to take us to the floor of the hospital where Ethan is waiting," Marshall said.

"This little room goes places? How is this possible?"

Marshall laughed.

"I think for now just take my word for it, we're going to see Ethan. I'll have to find an elevator diagram on the Internet so I can explain it to you."

Jalal nodded. He had no idea what Marshall was talking about. He bent down to Russell.

"We are going someplace Russell. At least that is what Marshall has said."

The door opened and they were on the 9th floor. Jalal looked out and his eyes got wide.

"We ARE someplace else," he said.

Marshall took hold of the kid's arm and they walked down the hallway. They stopped in front of the door to Ethan's room.

"Stay here a minute," he said.

Ethan was sleeping when Marshall quietly slipped back into his room. He checked to be sure and then snuck back to the door.

"I'm going to take Russell in and have him wake Ethan," Marshall said. "Then I'll come and get you."

Jalal grinned from ear to ear. "Eee-than will be much surprised," he said.

Marshall took the dog by his collar and led him into the room. When they were still several feet from the bed Russell became very excited. He could see his master and began struggling ahead. Marshall lost his grip on the collar and Russell bounded up to the bed and jumped up on it, landing on Ethan's stomach.

Ethan yelled and sat up looking startled. Then he realized what had happened and he grabbed the dog and hugged him tightly.

"Oh my God, Russell, you're alive boy, you're alive."

Ethan was crying and hugging the dog. Russell was lapping at his face and climbing onto him. Marshall was smiling and crying at the same time.

"Russell, I can't believe you're here!" he said. "Marshall how did you do this?"

"I know the right people," he said. He trotted over to the door and opened it. There stood Jalal sporting a ten thousand watt smile.

"Eee-than!" he said and ran to the bed. He jumped up on the bed with Russell and the three of them turned into one big pile of legs and arms and bodies. Everyone was hugging and crying and laughing at the same time.

Ethan reached out to Marshall and pulled him onto the pile.

"I should have known," he said. "Leave it up to you to do the impossible."

"It's the only way I could see to get you back," Marshall said.

Ethan hugged his friend and kissed him on the cheek. "I'm back Marshall... I'm back."

The next hour was chaos. Doctors and nurses and physical therapists came and went when they heard of the visitors. Jalal entertained them with his stories of defeating the bad men and Russell stayed put right on Ethan's bed, not moving one inch away from him.

Finally things calmed down and Ethan said to Marshall, "Tell me how you did this?"

Marshall related how Harry had helped and how Senator Johnson had pulled all the right strings to get it done.

"Russell is now retired and is officially your dog, and Jalal has a permanent visa and your parents have been approved to be his official host family. He's coming to Wisconsin with us as soon as you're ready to get out of this place."

Ethan was dumbstruck. "Go get the nurse. I want to double my therapy sessions."

Marshall couldn't get the smile off his face.

The boys stayed with Ethan late into the evening. They had dinner with him in the hospital cafeteria. Usually he'd been eating in his room but he wanted to go to the dining room so they all could eat together.

Jalal pushed him in a wheelchair and marveled at the vehicle.

"Jalal likes this chair with wheels. It would be good for gathering goat dung for the fire."

"Tomorrow I'm going to start working on crutches," Ethan said. "And if everything goes well, I'll be ready to go home in a week or less."

"You think you can do that?" Marshall asked.

"I know I can."

They all hugged goodbye finally late in the evening. Marshall had made arrangements with Harry to bring Jalal and Russell home with him. They promised Ethan they'd be back early in the morning.

They had a hard time to get Russell to go with them but finally the dog went along. When they got to Harry's place after a bus ride Jalal was noticeably tired. He was stumbling and Marshall knew he'd been on the road home for a long time. They talked for a short time with Harry and then went upstairs to

Marshall's room.

Harry had moved a second bed into the room for Jalal. He looked at the bed and then at Marshall.

"Jalal has never slept on such a bed," he said.

"What? You've never slept on a bed?"

"I have slept with my brother on the floor of our hut and when my family was killed I slept with the goats and then on the floor of Eee-than and Stew-arts hut. I had a nice soft mat when I slept on the floor of Eee-than's hut. The last months I have slept in a cave with Ru-sell."

"Well this bed is all for you. Get undressed and try it."

Jalal took off his shoes and socks and then his shirt and shorts. He looked at Marshall when it came to his boxers.

"You can leave them on," he said.

Marshall showed him how to pull the blankets back and he did and then lay on the bed. A smile appeared on his face.

"It is like sleeping on a new lamb."

Marshall laughed until his belly hurt.

"*Masaul Kazir*" "Good night" he said.

"Masaul whatever," Marshall said.

Russell jumped up and snuggled down with Jalal and soon he was snoring. Marshall lay awake for a minute and thought about the day.

"Ethan is coming home," he thought to himself. "He's coming home."

68

The next morning they had breakfast and Marshall realized that Jalal needed more clothes. The few items he had needed to be washed. Harry volunteered to drive them to a mall so they could shop for clothes.

Harry stayed with Russell in the parking lot while the boys went inside. Jalal was wide-eyed as they walked the halls past dozens of stores full of everything one could imagine.

"What do you think of this place?" Marshall asked.

"Jalal has never seen such things. How can there be so many wonderful things?"

"Each store has a different type of stuff," Marshall said, "Look at this store, it has electronic things, like TV, Ipods, PC's and Laptops."

Jalal looked in the window. "People can buy these things?"

Marshall nodded.

"What does one do with a PC?"

Marshall realized the kid had no idea what all of this stuff was. He smiled. "I'll teach you all about it."

They went to a clothing store and Jalal stood staring at the hundreds of shirts and trousers and piles of shoes. Marshall helped him pick out some more tee shirts and shorts and a pair of jeans. He got more boxers and then stopped by a display of sandals. He turned to Marshall.

"Jalal knows these shoes," he said.

"You want some of those?"

"It would be okey dokey?"

"Yeah, it would be okey dokey."

Ethan was in one of the physical therapy rooms when they arrived. Jalal was wearing a new striped tee shirt, a pair of baggy plaid shorts and his sandals. Ethan smiled when he saw him.

"You look just like an American already," he said.

Jalal smiled brilliantly.

"You like my new duds?"

Ethan looked at Marshall.

"You taught him a new word?"

Marshall grinned.

"Might as well get him speaking the language."

They watched Ethan work and then after he'd cleaned up they all went to the cafeteria and had lunch. Ethan was now able to get his shower and walked on crutches to the cafeteria.

They got slices of pizza and Jalal was overjoyed with the new food. He washed down three huge slices with Coke.

"How can so many wonderful things be?" he said.

"Oh you've just begun to find out wonderful things," Ethan said.

Russell sat next to Ethan and laid his head on his lap. Ethan rubbed the dog's ears and smiled at his little group.

Marshall saw the difference in Ethan's eyes. They sparkled like they used to and his mood was now upbeat. His cheeks were rosy and he smiled nearly all the time. There was no doubt now, he was on his way back.

Ethan worked like a maniac in the gym and got stronger and stronger. His wounds healed and his scars got less angry looking and became less noticeable.

He moved from crutches to two canes and a few days later he graduated to one cane. His arm was healed and he'd been building it up with weights to get it back to its old strength.

Marshall, Russell and Jalal spent every day at the hospital and soon became friends with many of the other patients. They loved talking to the boys and petting Russell. When Ethan rested after a long workout they'd make the rounds and visit other patients who were waiting to see them each day.

Jalal was very popular and the other patients smiled and laughed at his stories. Russell sat and let them pet him while Jalal entertained. They were very popular and brightened a lot of days for the injured soldiers.

69

The day was not far off when Ethan would be able to leave the hospital and work with a physical therapist at home. Two mornings later Marshall and Jalal and Russell were just opening the door to Ethan's room when an officer came walking out. He said hello to them and walked on.

Ethan was sitting on the edge of the bed in his shorts and tee shirt.

"Who was that guy?"

"That was a Lt. Colonel who is my boss."

"What was he here for?"

"Marshall, I'm going to stay in the Marines but I'll be on new duty. They have agreed to send me to college and when I'm finished I'm going to spend 20 years in the corps."

"Twenty years! Looking for bombs?"

"No, I'm going to college and then to medical school. I'm going to become a surgeon. Without good doctors I wouldn't have my legs. I want to help others who are hurt and help save lives. The Colonel just told me that the Marines are willing to pay for my education in return for my service."

"Holy smokes Ethan. You're going to be a doctor?"

Ethan grinned.

"I guess so, if I'm smart enough. But first we've got to get me home so I can start looking into school openings."

"I'm ready as soon as they let you go from here," Marshall said.

"Well, let's get packed up then."

"What? When can you leave?"

"Tomorrow," he said.

"Tomorrow?"

"I'm getting out of here tomorrow," he said.

"No way! Oh man, that's great. So we're going home tomorrow?"

"If you can get everything arranged."

"Holy smokes, that's pretty short notice," Marshall said.

Ethan looked at him.

"You know Marshall, I couldn't have done this without you. You never gave up on me."

"Friends never quit on friends Ethan. If you'd quit on me in Canada I wouldn't be here. I couldn't quit on you."

They hugged hard.

"Okay so now you have to work your magic and get us home," Ethan said.

"You could have given me a bit more notice," Marshall said grinning.

"The guy who brought me back from the depths of depression, got people to look for Russell and Jalal and brought them here from the mountains of Afghanistan doesn't think he can arrange a few airplane tickets?"

"I didn't say I couldn't do it, I said it was short notice. Of course I can do it."

"We are going to Weees-consin?" Jalal asked.

"Yes, you're going to become a Wisconsin Badger."

"What is badger?"

Marshall explained the badger. Jalal nodded knowingly.

"Jalal is badger. Jalal is brave like badger."

Marshall called Harry who made some calls and in no time they had reservations on a flight the next day to Madison. He called Senator Johnson's office and thanked them for all their help.

At the end of the day Marshall and Jalal took the bus to Harry's place. Ethan talked the nurses into letting Russell stay the night at the hospital. Ethan could get around on his own now and he wanted to go around and say goodbye to all the friends he'd made.

Harry took Marshall and Jalal to a steak house and they feasted on big steaks and French fries and all the trimmings. It was obvious that he was going to miss his young charges.

When they got back to Harry's the boys went upstairs to go to bed. Marshall had one last call to make.

"Hey, it's Marshall, how's it going?" he said to Ethan's mom.

"Everything's fine here honey, how are you guys doing?"

"We're all great. I've got news."

"What is it?"

"You need to be at the airport tomorrow at about noon."

"Oh my, Marshall, you mean...?'

"I'm bringing Ethan home."

ABOUT THE AUTHOR

Dan Bomkamp has made his home in the Wisconsin River valley all his life with the exception of his college years in La Crosse. He has been an avid hunter and fisherman his whole life. For many years he was in the sporting goods industry and began writing in the 80s for outdoor magazines. He is active in the Foreign Exchange Student program having hosted 33 boys from 13 countries over the years. Golden Retrievers have also been a big part of his life. He had at least one Golden sharing his home for 33 years. He lives in Muscoda with his cat, Tigger and his Boston Terrier, Buster.

Check out his website: www.danbomkamp.com

Or you can email him: danbomkamp@live.com